Daisy's Journey

Fiona Murphy

Fisher King Publishing

Fisher King Publishing
The Old Barn
York Road
Thirsk
YO7 3AD
England

fisherkingpublishing.co.uk

For my beloved late husband
for his belief and encouragement.

Acknowledgements

Immense gratitude to all my family and friends who exhorted me through the years to write stories.

Particular appreciation to Joanna Keenlyside for her inspirational input for the cover, to Maxine Linnell who helped me make sense of my ideas, Jo Catling for her input and prayers and Sue Sandham for her grammatical assistance!

Thanks especially to Fisher King for giving this book a chance to be published and also to Artus Digital for the pre-edit.

Chapter 1 – First Days

Daisy hurriedly stuffed the remainder of her clothes into the top of her travel bag then sat on it to close the zip. She took a final look around her empty room, a dull ache spreading through her heart. Leaving was the last thing she wanted to do. She recalled the recent conversations.

'What do you mean we're moving again?' Daisy had asked, feeling the colour drain from her face.

'Dad's had a transfer and it will be great to be nearer Gran,' Mum had smiled. 'We've found a school for Rosie too and I've found a part-time job.'

Daisy hadn't smiled back. She was used to Dad getting transferred – company policy, apparently – but she hated it. Every time it meant changes for her. As for Gran, she'd just gone on a cruise, so that worked... not.

'Of course.' Daisy knew from experience there was no point arguing, so she'd worked hard to keep her voice calm even though inside she'd been screaming. So you've got it all sorted, she'd thought; you, Dad, and my sister! Good for you, but I don't want to go! I've told you a million times, I hate moving! It wasn't like they took any notice of her anyway. She'd checked the new place, Waterside, on Google Maps. It was over an hour away. No-one else from her sixth form or even anyone she knew would be going there. It would be awful, just like before. She knew it.

She felt sick even thinking about when the panic

attacks had begun. Her parents knew how awful it had been and now they wanted her to make yet another new start!

Daisy had forced a smile then headed upstairs. She'd flung herself on her bed and messaged the one friend she still had.

"Hi Jonno." Nothing. She knew he'd message back when he could though. It was because of the panic attacks that she'd met Jonno, her first real friend at Meadow Lane, and he always responded. They had a kind of pact about it. They'd met at the ultra-humiliating Pupil Wellbeing Therapy Group. She'd only agreed to go as it meant missing PE. She had sat there, arms crossed, hugging her knees. She'd glanced at the gaunt face next to her that first day and had been horrified to see tears silently sliding down his pale cheeks. She'd never seen a boy cry before. He'd caught her looking at him, and seeing the compassion in her eyes, had given an attempt at a smile. They'd soon become close friends, both hating the sessions, both with different issues. Her phone buzzed.

"Hi Daze."

"Hi Jonno. How are you and where in the world?"

"Great and Greek Islands, also great. How about you?"

"Euch! Today's been gross – the grossest. Can you believe my parents are moving us again! Honestly, what are they like? You're the only one who seems to understand. Why do you have to be so far away? I really need you."

"Oh Daze, I'd love to see you too. I have so much to

tell you. The fellow crew members are great and well, I'll keep you posted. Hey, I should get leave dates soon. I'll let you know and hopefully we can meet up.

Meanwhile, spill it, talk me through your gross day."

Following a long messaging session with Jonno, she'd felt better.

He had said she could message him whenever and even if he couldn't reply immediately, he'd promised to read her message and get back when he could. It was, they decided, the next best thing to chatting.

Jonno was so easy to chat to. He was really open with his feelings.

At the second session of the totally embarrassing Wellbeing Group, he'd said to her, 'You'll never guess why I'm here.'

Daisy hadn't been sure how to respond, but he'd gone on anyway. 'Caught puking in the bushes. I know, I know, it's meant to be girls who have the eating disorders.' He'd looked down. 'Girls aren't the only ones with body image issues, you know.'

Daisy had stayed silent. He clearly needed to talk.

'I'm gay, my parents don't know. Yeah, everyone's meant to be cool with that stuff now, but not everyone's dad is in the army. I know the military don't discriminate anymore, but if you've been brought up with all the jibes...'

Jonno and Daisy had soon become besties.

She missed him.

He had helped her when a boy had asked her out but

made a laughing stock of her when he discovered she played the harp and liked jazz music.

She had helped Jonno through telling his parents he was gay and that he wanted to go into the entertainment industry not the army. He had left straight after GCSEs to go to dance school.

It had been so hard when he left but at least they'd been able to stay in touch easily. Now he'd landed a job on a cruise ship and it was much more difficult for them to communicate across time-zones, but she knew he'd message her when he could.

He was helping her now too. Knowing he was okay talking about stuff meant she felt he really understood when she told him how she was feeling. Not like Mum and Dad. Anyone would think they were stuck in the Victorian era. Jonno had laughed on the phone when she'd said that.

'Hang on though,' he'd replied, 'think about it. Didn't you say your dad was partly raised by his Victorian gran when his mum had been sick? Maybe that's the only way they know?'

Daisy had thought about this. She'd crept downstairs and found Mum in the kitchen, hoping they could have a chat.

'Yes?' Mum had said, turning away to get plates from the cupboard.

'I was just going to ask about Sixth Form. If I could stay and commute from Gran's, I could get a bus?'

'It would cost far too much!' Dad had countered,

appearing in the doorway. 'Anyway, think of your music. I know Meadow Lane let you take the A-level early, but Waterside has an excellent reputation for music so it's ideal for the Diploma.'

Daisy had nodded, walked out and slunk upstairs again.

However hard she tried, they simply wouldn't (or maybe couldn't) seem to understand what was important to her.

"Never mind my education. I need a manual on how to educate my parents into the 21st century," she'd messaged, hoping Jonno might have a few tips.

The inevitable had happened though – today they were moving.

She closed her bedroom door for the last time.

Daisy looked around a bit as they drove into Waterside and noticed a market square: from there the town appeared to descend to a lake. Nearby sat the college. It looked uninspiring.

Chapter 2 – Dismal Days

Daisy had only been at Waterside College for a week and was in awe of everyone. She'd registered her name on Waterside's social media site but hadn't yet dared post anything. The only glimmer on her bleak horizon was the music. She loved music and had learned piano as a child, but the harp was her favourite instrument. Waterside offered the harp. She wanted to play the jazz harp. Her first harp teacher played that as well as teaching them classical harp. Her parents had insisted she choose classical harp. She still preferred jazz music but had fallen in love with the harp as an instrument.

She had been given instructions to locate and label the harp she was renting from the college. In the first music room, she heard a harp playing and stopped at the door. Was it a recording or live music? Her phone alarm beeped. Lunch break was almost over. She sped into the music room next door, quickly found her harp and tagged it with the label. English next – Shakespeare. Had she put her book in? She ferreted in her bag before heading off to class. Daisy tried to concentrate on the text of 'Romeo and Juliet' but her mind kept drifting. That harp music...

'Daisy Davidson!' boomed the tutor. 'Can you tell us your thoughts on the opposition from the families to this romance?' This was the one topic she'd glanced through last night so thankfully she could answer.

An hour later, she was laden with a stack of new poetry

books. The tutor seemed to assume she had time to run errands. Not like she had anything else to do though. But perhaps, she wondered, recalling the music she'd heard earlier, perhaps she wasn't the only harpist here at Waterside? She hummed the melody she'd heard, the soft chords plucked from the instrument. Her heart seemed to fizz. Maybe Mum and Dad were right after all? Maybe here she'd be able to develop her harp playing and, dare she hope, more? Perhaps a new friend who shared her interest? Knowing her luck though, the mystery harp player would be a teacher!

A shadow loomed across her path. She looked up and tumbled into a guy. His music case flew out of his hand and the pile of poetry books hit the floor.

'Sorry, sorry, I didn't...' she began. Noticing he looked really fit, she knelt down, her face flaring, and started scrabbling to collect his music scores from the floor. They were harp scores. Could he be the harp player she'd heard? She was such a klutz! Why oh why did she have to crash into him? She glanced up. His gorgeous milk chocolate eyes seemed amused. He knelt and joined her, and together they restored the scores and books to orderly stacks.

Clutching the poetry books, she turned to walk away.

'Sorry, really sorry...' She threw the words over her shoulder. She had to escape before she embarrassed herself even more.

'Hey, don't worry.' His deep voice was unusually accented. 'You picked up my harp scores, grazie.'

Gingerly, Daisy glanced back. He was still there. He grinned at her and then was gone, loping up the hallway. Daisy stood as if rooted to the ground. Then she heard a group of people approaching. She tried to move on but they blocked her way. They were all dressed alike in the latest mini skirts and crop tops.

'Hah!' One blond streak squawked at her, high heels tapping sharply as she minced past. 'Don't think for one second you stand a chance with him, he's far too classy for you.'

The gaggle of girls sniggered their way past.

Daisy felt crushed. She'd often been teased in the past. She loathed the way she looked – frizzy auburn hair, a crazy number of freckles, not exactly skinny, and then there was her clumsiness. She was used to this kind of comment but that didn't mean it hurt any less. Her parents had shrugged when she'd told them as a child.

"Sticks and stones..." they'd quoted at her, but her heart told her words could hurt more than sticks and stones.

'Ignore her,' a cheery voice called from behind. Daisy turned, relaxing as she realised it was Grace Bloom, the only person who had offered her a few friendly words on her first day. She looked up to see Grace's hazel eyes shining kindly at her. The girl tipped her head to the side, her long brown hair flopping over one shoulder.

'Sad, really, but Lucy's mind seems full of junk like that! Here, let me give you a hand with those books.'

Daisy smiled her gratitude as Grace took half the pile. Together they stored them in the staff room and made their way out of school into the breezy afternoon. Grace waved as they parted ways at the gate.

Moments later, she caught Daisy up.

'Would you like to try out the new ice-cream parlour sometime? It opened yesterday near the lake. My brother took his girlfriend last night and by all accounts they do the most delicious caramel sundae.'

Daisy grinned. 'Sure, which day's good for you?' They agreed on next Thursday as they both finished early that afternoon.

Daisy made her way home feeling cheered and more lighthearted. A verse she had once heard in school assembly came into her mind: "An anxious heart weighs a man down but a kind word cheers him." Maybe it was true. She passed the market square on her way back and decided to buy her mum some Michaelmas daisies at the last flower stall still trading. They were her mum's favourite; her parents joked that it was why they had named her Daisy.

Mum had been tired recently, what with the house move then Rosie having chickenpox. Well, they wanted to relocate! Daisy grimaced at the ungracious thought flashing through her head, reminding her of the resentment she still felt about leaving Meadow Lane. She knew she could've been more helpful but it was so awful moving. Now though, it was possible she could make some new friends. There was lightness in her step for the first time since the move.

'Hi!' Daisy called, unlocking the door and fussing

Muddle their mongrel dog as she went in. There was no response. She went into the back garden. It seemed colder in the few minutes since coming in and she rubbed her arms to warm them. She looked up at the sky and noticed clouds were gathering. She took out her phone; she hadn't heard it buzz but there were several missed calls and a text from Dad. A glacial chill swept through her as she read it.

Chapter 3 – Difficult Days

Daisy grabbed her purse, flung her satchel down, ran to the garage and dragged out her bike. She'd hardly used it recently as she could sometimes borrow the car and she was relieved that the tyres weren't flat. She shoved her helmet on and sped out into the now grey and blustery afternoon up the road towards Waterside General Hospital. She burst through the hospital doors into the foyer with its distinctive smell of disinfectant and saw her father pacing up and down outside the ward opposite. His ashen face mirrored the sky.

'There was an explosion at Rosie's school...' he began.

Daisy had never seen her dad cry, but as he leaned to hug her, a single glassy droplet slid down his cheek. She took his hand and looked at him.

'Mum was in the Resources Room. The boiler in the cupboard next door exploded. She said she heard a violent shuddering and then the wall shattered. Shards of wood and plaster flew into her. They went in her eyes...' His voice cracked. 'The doctor said tiny splinters had pierced both her corneas. They're operating now to try and save her sight.'

Wordlessly, Daisy found them seats near a vending machine. She sat watching dull brown liquid gurgle and steam into paper cups as countless agitated people sought to distract themselves. Dad carried on pacing.

'I bought Mum some flowers earlier...'

Her father's voice broke through the swirling sea of emotion bubbling up.

'Rosie's at after-school club. They close at 6 p.m. I want to stay. Will you collect her?'

Dad's voice sounded shocked even though he was trying to organise the practicalities. She nodded and he finally sat down.

Daisy dug in her pocket and finding just enough money she bought him a cup of strong sweet tea and some coffee for herself. He needed her to be responsible for him but it was all too much, like being sucked into a whirlpool. She sipped the bitter scalding coffee. Questions began to leap about her mind like ensnared creatures seeking escape. What would she tell Rosie? Was there anything to eat in the house? Would her parents be back at all tonight? Should she prepare the house in any way in case... in case... Daisy couldn't let herself even think about her mum's sight, not while she was trying to help Dad and look after Rosie. She stood up as a nurse approached them.

'You can come and see your wife now. The doctor will explain how things are,' she said, addressing Daisy's dad but beckoning to them both.

Mum was lying down in bed with her eyes bandaged. She looked pale and somehow fragile – not at all like the in-control Mum Daisy knew.

'The operation was a success so we're confident her sight will be saved.' Waves of relief rippled through Daisy at the doctor's words.

'However,' the doctor continued, turning to Mum, 'the bandages need to stay on for a few days and you will need lots of rest. I'd like you to stay overnight, but all being well, you can go home tomorrow. We'll arrange an out-patient appointment for Friday.'

Daisy wheeled her bike home, feeling too shaken up to cycle. She collected Rosie and they walked back to the hospital. She was glad to be able to tell her Mum was going to be okay. Dad drove them all home, picking up a takeaway. It was a strange evening without Mum. None of them said very much that night, not even Rosie, who usually had verbal diarrhoea. No-one had realised how different it would feel without Mum fussing around, chatting about her day, asking them about theirs, providing food, clearing away and reminding them to do things they were hoping to avoid.

Finally Dad said, 'It'll be wonderful when Mum's back tomorrow but I shall need you both to help out.'

Daisy felt a stab of worry. What about her Thursday arrangement with Grace? She dropped her eyes and said nothing. Mum was lying in hospital and still couldn't see.

'Daisy,' Dad continued, 'you can take Mum's car and collect Rosie from school. Rosie, you can help Daisy with tea after school each day for a while.'

After they'd eaten, Dad and Rosie cleared away and Daisy walked Muddle. After Rosie's homework was done, they all went to bed early. Daisy sprawled flat out on her bed and dragged floppy Ted from underneath. She needed him tonight. She'd had no idea how exhausting it was taking care of everything Mum usually did. How would she fit in all the jobs on top of college and still have time for friends?

She messaged Jonno.

"It's been a horrid day. Mum had an accident and may not be able to see for ages, if at all. I don't know how we're going to manage without her." She stopped for a moment as the tears fell. She hadn't felt she could cry when she was with Dad. Eventually, she picked up her phone again and sent another message. "It's not all bad though – looks like I may have made a new friend, Grace. We're going to an ice-cream parlour later this week hopefully. I'll let you know how it goes. Hope you're having fun and can message soon. Love Daze xx"

Chapter 4 – Different Days

Daisy skipped her last lecture on Tuesday and rushed to the supermarket to buy tea. She picked Rosie up from her swimming lesson then hurried back to get tea ready before Dad returned with Mum. When Mum arrived home that evening, her bandages were still on. Muddle was so delighted to see her; Daisy had to hold him back from jumping up as Dad led her down the hall. Daisy felt her eyes fill when they passed the stand where the Michaelmas daisies sat in a vase. Her Mum couldn't see them. She bent down to fuss Muddle until she could be sure no-one would notice the tears threatening to fall. She wanted to be strong for all of them. It was hard though.

For tea, Mum just wanted soup with a straw and bread. She she said she was worried she'd drop her food otherwise. Afterwards, Dad said he'd try and get a message to Gran. They didn't want to spoil her holiday but she'd want to know about the accident.

'I'm taking Wednesday and Thursday as holiday to be with Mum,' Dad announced after the call. 'Gran will be back next week to help out. That's when her cruise ends.'

Daisy felt her heart lift. She was free to go to the café and maybe she'd even have time to visit the music room after school. Perhaps she'd mention the mystery harpist to Gran. Gran had been on her side when she'd showed an interest in the jazz harp. Daisy knew her grandfather had played it, but Mum never liked it. It had meant late nights going to listen to him as a teenager rather than being out with friends. Dad preferred classical music and thought she'd have a better career being classically trained. Daisy thought this opinion was out of the Ark but hadn't said so – yet.

She jumped up and offered to clear the table so Rosie could begin her homework. While she was stacking the dishwasher, her mind wandered back to the mystery harpist. She'd been looking out for him since Monday. Would she ever see him again? She couldn't ask anyone about him as she didn't even know his name yet. She was being ridiculous, getting obsessed. She didn't want to turn into some kind of weird stalker. His gorgeous image with its lopsided grin popped into her head. Hmm. Maybe she could ask Grace about him at the ice-cream parlour tomorrow?

The ice-cream parlour turned out to be a café too. It was set back from the path that led to the lake. Outside there were round tables, most of them occupied and sheltered from the evening sun, some under a tree and some shaded by pink and yellow striped awnings. To the left sat a huge stone pizza oven and Daisy heard some kind of guitar music drifting out as she stood waiting. Grace hadn't arrived yet. Daisy checked her watch. She had the time right. She hoped she'd turn up and wondered how long she should wait. Ten minutes then text her, or would that seem needy? Daisy looked around. No sign yet. She turned towards the lake and noticed a small sailing boat some distance from the shore.

'Hi!' Grace called, hurrying down.

'Soz, waylaid.'

Daisy wondered how or with what but didn't ask.

The two girls went into the café where a rainbow of ice-cream in huge tubs greeted them. The lady at the counter was scooping generous portions into sugar cones dipped in chocolate. Two children with excited faces, whose noses just reached the top of the counter, waited eagerly.

'I'm definitely going for the caramel sundae.' Grace pointed at a tub containing luscious honey-coloured ice-cream swirled with caramel and studded with white chocolate chips.

'Raspberry sorbet for me, please.' Daisy chose one scoop in a tiny tub. She didn't want to look greedy and it was constant battle trying to keep slim-ish.

The café was buzzing so, taking their ices, they headed for the only free table outside that overlooked the lake.

'Good week?' Grace asked between greedy slurps.

'Er, yes.' Daisy wasn't sure she could say anything about Mum's accident. She didn't really know Grace that well yet and she hated being upset in front of people. 'How about you?'

'Okay,' Grace said, 'if you don't count getting a warning from my tutor for handing in another essay late. I mean, I know they need to be on time but, well, Dad was home on leave. He's in the Forces so he and Mum don't have that much time together. The rest of us try to make sure we pick up jobs at home so they can go out when he's back. I've been extra busy. So okay, maybe I could have spent less time on my art and more on the essay but well, that's me.' Grace shrugged. So Daisy wasn't alone in doing extra jobs at home. She sighed.

'Are you sure it was a good week? You sound tired.' Grace's concerned look and the way she'd unreservedly talked about her family meant Daisy felt she could tell Grace the truth about her own week.

'Well, actually, Mum had an accident this week and...'

'What happened?' interrupted Grace.

'A boiler exploded at the school where she works. Shards went into her eyes and she needed an operation. The doctor says her sight should be okay but she still has bandages on. She has a hospital appointment tomorrow to see if they can be removed. Meanwhile, it's all hands helping out.' Daisy looked away as a bubble of emotion rose in her throat. She gripped her tub of ice-cream with one hand, leaving the plastic spoon dripping in the other. Grace reached out her hand and gently squeezed Daisy's.

'If you need any help with anything, shopping, whatever, please let me know.'

Daisy nodded. 'Thanks...' she began, then stopped. She'd noticed Grace's attention had drifted and the sailing dinghy had landed. The helmsman was securing it and looked familiar. Daisy felt her face go hot as she watched him walking up the beach. Her pulse began to race. It was him – the mystery harpist! Turning away quickly, she looked towards Grace but was dismayed to see her waving at the sailor. He started walking towards them.

'Hey,' he called, 'how's it going?'

'Do...' Daisy swallowed, 'do you know him, Grace?'

'Giorgio? Why sure, I know him from church, his family moved here not long ago. This is their ice-cream parlour and café.'

Daisy gulped and took a mouthful of her sorbet. Just as he arrived, she began coughing and spluttering as it went down the wrong way. Her face flamed crimson and she dashed to the loo. Again, she thought, again! She'd made a fool of herself again in front of him. She felt the hot tears of embarrassment rising and splashed her cheeks with cold water to cool them. She wouldn't cry.

Daisy took her time, feeling sure Giorgio would be gone soon. She edged out of the loo and had a look. Thankfully, only Grace was at their table. As she crept out she heard the deeply accented voice of Giorgio.

'Hey, are you okay now?'

She couldn't bring herself to look at him. 'Fine, thanks, er...' she muttered, scooting to the table then calling back, 'Just, er, got to go.' She grabbed her bag and signalled to Grace that she needed to leave.

Feeling bad about leaving her friend, Daisy glanced back moments later and noticed Giorgio had joined Grace. Why oh why, she asked herself, did she have to do these things and then behave so foolishly? Grace would have just laughed it off. Why couldn't she be more like her? Some hope of Grace wanting to stay friends with her now. And as for acquainting herself with Giorgio, no chance!

Daisy dumped her bag in the porch to open the door, then forgetting it, she clomped upstairs and sank onto her bed, burying her face in her pillow. Hot salty rivulets ran down her cheeks and she hugged herself tight as if to squeeze away the hurt she felt inside. Why did these things always happen to her? Why couldn't she be cool, sophisticated or effortlessly stylish like other girls? Her mum usually told her just to stop being oversenstive. That was easy to say, she thought bitterly, when it wasn't her!

The doorbell rang, interrupting her self-pity fest. Who could that be? No-one was expected as far as she knew. Dad had taken Mum and Rosie out for tea to a local pub with Muddle so she'd need to answer it. She could ignore it but it could be important, and she was supposed to be being responsible now. She hastily rubbed her face with the pillowcase.

Daisy did a double-take when she opened the door to both Grace and Giorgio. How did they even know where she lived?

'Hey, how's it going? We saw you head this way and noticed your bag. We wanted to ask if you'd like to join us out on the lake this evening?' Giorgio asked.

Grace nodded.

Daisy was staggered. They weren't laughing at her and hadn't even mentioned earlier at the ice-cream café. Could they really still want to offer her friendship?

'Well,' she faltered, 'what time?'

'We were thinking of setting off about six to be back around eight. We could all go for pizza at the café afterwards if that suits?' Grace suggested.

'Sounds great, where shall I meet you?'

'At the jetty at say five forty-five?'

Giorgio confirmed with a nod and they left.

Daisy wasn't at all sure about boating or a return to the café. Would she make a fool of herself yet again? Well, even if she did, she wasn't going to let this friendship opportunity pass her by. She could make a mini picnic with tiny jam tarts, she thought. That would be a treat for Rosie too when they came back, and Mum and Dad also loved them. She could take some of Gran's elderflower champagne as well.

Chapter 5 – Day's Eve

As she neared the jetty, Daisy wondered again why she'd agreed to the boating. What if she fell in and made an even bigger fool of herself? Why did she do this? She was always thinking of what could go wrong. She wanted to have friends though, and Gran had told her it was good to make the effort to build friendships. That's why she'd agreed.

She stepped onto the jetty and called 'Hi'.

Giorgio and Grace stood near the end next to a rowing boat painted red, white and green with a Greek flag.

'Hey, how's it going? Do you like the boat? My dad insisted if the family had a boat it should be painted in the colours of the Italian flag and sport a Greek one to represent our joint nationality. Cool, hey?'

Daisy smiled. Inwardly she let out a breath she hadn't realised she'd been holding. Rowing, not sailing – that was good. She was glad she'd at least had a bit of practise from taking Rosie on the park boating lake last year.

Daisy handed him a small basket. 'Refreshments!' she offered.

'Hey, most encouraging,' Giorgio grinned. Daisy wasn't sure what he meant exactly but decided to concentrate on boarding and let it go.

After a few wobbles, she managed to sit down. Grace got in and took the oars.

'We're heading to that tiny island partway across the

lake?' Giorgio asked, looking in the direction behind him.

Grace nodded. After a short while she passed over the oars.

Soon, Giorgio's strong strokes were putting a good distance between them and the shore. Daisy felt a lazy late summer breeze gently caressing her bare arms as he pushed the craft through the water. After a while, he offered Daisy the oars.

'Oh, I'm not sure... I mean...' It was one thing taking Rosie out but what if she tipped this boat?

'Hey, have a go.'

'Maybe Grace...?' Daisy looked over to Grace. She had taken out a small sketchbook and was intent on sketching. 'Maybe not.'

The boat wobbled as they changed places. She nearly toppled until she felt Giorgio's firm hand steadying her arm. She was glad she was looking down so he couldn't see her blush.

Daisy surprised herself by enjoying her turn but was also relieved to pass back the oars.

'Will this do?' Giorgio asked, startling Grace from her sketching as he landed them in a sandy cove on the north shore.

Together they pulled the boat up and secured her before heading for shade under some tall pines skirting the edge of the bay. Grace unpacked the basket then to Daisy's surprise, Giorgio held his hand up.

'Anyone mind if I say a word of thanks?' Daisy wondered what he meant, so kept silent.

'Hey God, we really appreciate this food and the opportunity for fun times with friends. Amen.'

Daisy had never heard grace before meals spoken so freely and without formality before. Perhaps God was all for alfresco eating and having a good time? She hadn't ever really thought of Him in that way. When of course she thought of Him at all, which to be fair was rarely.

Pop! Grace giggled as the cork on Gran's elderflower champagne flew into the boat and fizzy puddles appeared in the sand. Giorgio poured it into the paper cups Daisy had brought and took a mouthful.

'Hey, wow! I haven't sampled this since I was last in Italy.'Daisy glowed at Giorgio's clear pleasure. Elderflower champagne was something her grandmother had taught her to make correctly, from showing Daisy how to gather the fragrant blooms in late spring to the bottling method. The three of them sat chatting easily, sipping and munching the tiny sweet blackberry tarts Daisy had brought.

'Did you make these?' asked Grace.

'Well, yes,' replied Daisy hesitantly, 'Mum's not been well recently, as you know, and so I thought she might appreciate a treat and we could have some too. Mum's not keen on cooking at the best of times but my Gran loves it, so we often had jam making sessions or pickling days. I grew to love it too. I know it's rather old–fashioned.'

'Hey, don't knock it,' countered Giorgio, 'it's totally the Italian way, and in Greece too. These taste amazing!'

Daisy dropped her head feeling her cheeks beginning

to glow, but this time her heart felt warm. She smiled back shyly.

'Is your mum any better?' Grace asked.

Daisy explained to Giorgio about the accident, struggling to hold the tears back. She saw the concern in his eyes.

'You will let me know if you need any help, won't you?' Grace reminded her.

She nodded, her voice quavering as she thanked her.

Daisy concentrated on watching their boat bobbing until she felt calmer, then lay back and wriggled her bare toes in the surf, letting the cool water ripple over them as tiny waves lapped the shore. She was dozing when Grace nudged her and pointed out a honeyed-pink light brushing the horizon.

'It's as if God's beginning to paint the sunset,' Grace said, delving into her pocket for her sketchbook. Too soon, it was time to head back.

Later, helping to pull the boat back up the pebbly shore, Daisy realised it'd been a long while since she'd felt so content. It was unusual for her to be relaxed this early in a friendship.

'Thanks you guys,' she said, her eyes shining, 'I really enjoyed this evening.'

'That's good,' said Grace, 'because we're hoping you'll be part of our team for the church boat race on Friday. This was a kind of practice. No pressure though.'

Daisy gulped. Not feeling sure about church or races, she hesitated. It amazed her following her experience of church years ago that such a place would even consider this kind of activity, but her desire to be with Giorgio and Grace gained the upper hand. 'I could give it a try,' she replied.

'Hey, excellent!' Giorgio punched the air and gave her a friendly hug. Daisy felt her heart quiver and her cheeks flame.

As they approached the café, woodsmoke curled from the pizza oven and a white-haired man of generous proportions raked the embers. Seeing Giorgio, he put the rake down and limped over.

'Hey, grab a table. I'll just be a minute.' Giorgio headed off inside.

Grace and Daisy studied the menu.

'My brother Zach says the garlic bread's amazing. Shall we share some?'

'Okay,' Daisy agreed. Grace loved her food. It was great to have a friend who was as much of a foodie as she was herself.

Giorgio reappeared.

'Hey, sorry guys, but my brother's had to go out, that's why Dad's doing the pizzas. They need my help. Catch you later.'

Disappointment clutched at Daisy's heart. She took a deep breath. They'd had a great evening and she could still enjoy a pizza with Grace. Don't make an idiot of yourself by letting anyone see you're upset, she instructed herself, studying the menu.

Daisy decided on the spicy calzone and Grace chose

a vegetarian pizza.

'Plus garlic bread to share?' Grace suggested.

'Well, er, okay.'

Such a different approach to food from the diet-crazed girls at Meadow Lane, thought Daisy. Grace didn't seem to be obsessed about her body image either.

There was no sign of Giorgio later and too soon it was time to leave. He might have known they'd have to go by now, she thought; he could have come and said bye. She didn't want Grace to realise how keen she was on him so she said nothing.

Back home, there was a dish left on the kitchen table with a note. Mum, Dad and Rosie had been pleased with the tarts. The dish was empty and Daisy noticed Muddle was surrounded by crumbs.

'That wouldn't have happened if Mum could have seen there were tarts left on the plate,' Daisy told him. Hopefully, the bandages would come off tomorrow and Mum would be able to see. It wasn't easy helping out.

How did young carers cope?

Daisy snuggled under her covers and thought about the race. It'd been fun but hard work rowing. She'd need to get a bit fitter, exercise more and cut out a few sweet treats. Not just to impress Giorgio, of course. Where had that thought come from? Although, she was definitely interested in Giorgio for more than his harp! Sleepily, she fetched out her phone and text Jonno. "Can't wait to tell you my news, message when you can."

Chapter 6 – Disappointing Days

'Mum's check-up has gone well. The bandages are off and her sight's coming back,' Dad called to Daisy as she made her way through the hall.

'Michaelmas daisies,' Mum said, beaming as she came into the kitchen. Daisy was pleased they were still blooming.

Mum needed more rest, so the weekend flew by as Daisy helped with chores at home, took Muddle out and ran Rosie to a party and back. She'd hoped Grace might text about meeting up somewhere with Giorgio but no joy.

'Urgh!' Daisy leaned over to silence the blare of the alarm clock. Monday – perhaps Giorgio would be in the music room again? She dressed in her favourite jeans and a black jumper; she always felt slimmer in that. She looked in the mirror and thought she looked a bit pale. It must be all this running around, she thought. Good job Gran was arriving soon. She hastily threw her turquoise necklace on and checked her reflection again. Better. She ran downstairs and scribbled a note to say she'd left early for college, grabbed a banana for breakfast and drove off.

At school, Daisy lingered in the music corridor until class but there was no sign of Giorgio, nor did she hear his harp. So much for all the dithering about what to wear! Not that she should dress just for him, of course. Grace messaged her to remind her about the boat race and let her know it would start at 6 p.m. Friday. "Meet at the lake, pizza after if you like?" Daisy messaged back: "Great." At least she'd see Giorgio then, although Friday felt a long way off. What if Dad needed her to be in for Mum or to pick up Rosie? He was often late on Fridays and Gran would need to go home by then. Impish thoughts tortured Daisy throughout the day with threats that she might not see Giorgio.

When she arrived home, she knew immediately Gran was there. The house was filled with the scent of apple and cinnamon; Gran must be baking one of her amazing pies, she thought. Daisy was enveloped in a hug and lightly dusted with flour as soon as she entered the kitchen. She hugged Gran back, then brushing off the flour and laughing, she was despatched with a cup of tea for Mum, returning to catch Gran indulging Muddle with a few scraps.

It was great to catch up with Gran, who was very reassuring about Mum and had some fun tales about her holiday. She'd be going home each evening though and she'd told Daisy she had a friend she'd met on holiday visiting at the weekend. Daisy was about to mention the mystery harpist when Rosie appeared.

'Dad?' Daisy began later when Rosie had gone to her art club. 'Will you need me around on Friday evening?'

'Well, we're due to visit Aunt May so we'll all be away for the weekend. Mum's keen to go now she's feeling better. It will be a nice break.'

'Can I stay here?'

'We'd rather you came.' Dad gave her one of his "please don't argue" looks.

'What?' Daisy pushed, 'Don't you trust me?'

'Of course we do,' said Dad, 'It's just we're not keen on you being here alone all weekend. Gran has a friend staying.'

Daisy knew she should be glad to go. Mum, still recovering, would love a weekend away, but why did Gran have to have a friend staying this weekend?

Daisy felt her heart clench. Grandpa had passed on only a few years ago. It was mean of her to want to deprive Gran of a new friendship. Daisy wanted to shout at Dad – so she was old enough to take on a cartful of responsibility running Rosie around, shopping and cleaning when it suited, but not to stay home alone for one weekend! She dug her nails into her hands, desperately clinging on to her temper. She felt horribly mean to be annoyed but she was so frustrated and disappointed. She would miss the boat race practice or to be more precise, a chance to see Giorgio, and Grace of course.

Conscious of a volcanic-style eruption mounting, she muttered something about taking Muddle out and left. A slate sky greeted her. As she paced along the bridleway, hot tears filled her eyes. Now she'd have to let her new friends down. She marched along, fighting a rising tide of fear. She was frightened that having to dip out on Friday would threaten her friendships. Salty rivulets coursed down her cheeks. She went to take out her phone to message Jonno, then realising she'd left it at home, she crept back.

Daisy tried to open the front door silently when she and Muddle arrived back. She stood in the hallway and listened. The house was quiet and dark. Good – she finally had some space to herself. They must have gone to collect Rosie and Gran must have gone home. It was lovely that Gran was helping but the house seemed so hectic. Ah – there was her phone on the table. She sat down to check for messages. There were none. She flopped across the table and let the tears fall, painful sobs escaping.

'Whatever is the matter?' Gran's voice sounded behind her.

Daisy sat up. 'Nothing,' she muttered, scrubbing her face. She hated anyone to see her cry.

'Oh Gran, I thought you'd gone home.'

'Well, I was in the garden but I'm still here. Now tell me what's happened to upset you so much, my lovely?' The kindness in Gran's voice tipped the burbling emotion and the waterfall of tears began to fall again. Daisy hid her face. Gran put her arm around her granddaughter's shoulders and said nothing until Daisy brushed away the tears and looked up.

'Is it friends or Mum?' Gran asked gently. Daisy nodded, not trusting herself to speak. She took a deep breath.

'You'll think I'm a stupid baby,' she began. Gran shook her head. 'I was upset about Mum and I just worry so much about friends, as you know.' Daisy stopped and looked at Gran. Gran nodded.

'I understand...' she began, 'but sometimes it helps to talk.' Gran lifted the cuff of her cardigan and showed Daisy a bruised arm with a large plaster near the wrist.

'Oh Gran. What happened?'

'I was tidying the bed near the verge after summer – you know how I like my gardening – anyway, a car whizzed by and out of nowhere, a stone flew up and caught my wrist. There's a nasty graze.'

'Are you okay?' Daisy asked.

'Oh yes, I washed it and am keeping it covered for now so it doesn't get knocked or dirty and infected, but I'll let the air to it soon. That's important for the healing. I often think hurt feelings are like that.'

'What do you mean?' Daisy asked.

'I think tears can be good, a sort of river to clean the wound, and then talking about things is like bringing air to the wound and can help the healing begin. The difficult thing though is feeling safe enough to let the tears and the talk do their work.'

'It's hard to feel safe,' Daisy said, her eyes filling again.

'I'm here if you need me. Remember, you've had a lot going on with Mum's injury. I know she's on the mend but sometimes it takes our hearts time to catch up with our heads.' Gran stopped. Daisy gave her a watery smile of thanks. It felt good to have someone understand without having to explain.

'By the way,' Gran continued, 'music is a good salve. How about that jazz harp you mentioned a while back, any progress?' Daisy sighed.

'Okay,' Gran said, turning to collect some plates, 'Point taken. Now, will you take this dog out from under my feet? I'm trying to stack the dishwasher and he's trying to feast on a second supper.'

Daisy grabbed Muddle's lead and took the dog off, messaging as she went. Gran was right. It would be good to talk and she did know someone she felt safe to talk to.

"Jonno, I need to talk to you. My parents are so infuriating. I want to tell you about my friend, Grace, and this guy I really like, Giorgio. They want me to go to an event but my family are insisting I go to my aunt's with them. How can I persuade them? You are always so good at sorting out these kinds of things. Pleeease message. Daze xx"

She shoved her phone back in her pocket. This always happened. There was always something – her clumsiness, family arrangements or some drama that meant she couldn't do what everyone else her age seemed to be able to do. Why couldn't she spend time with her friends instead of having to go with the family like a little kid?

Muddle stopped at a fallen tree, throwing earth up as he dug around its roots. Daisy felt the rough bark as she rested against the sturdy trunk waiting for him. Muddle gave up his quest and nuzzled her, pushing his muddy nose at her, inviting her to fuss him. She sank down, burying her face in his warm fur and sobbed some more. A rustling in the hedge alerted her and she looked up. She'd come farther along the path than she'd realised. This was unfamiliar territory. She clutched Muddle's collar tight. Who or what was in the undergrowth? She heard a throaty cough. Alarm stabbed at her heart. A foot appeared, rapidly followed by a head.

Grace emerged, snapping twigs that caught up in her jumper as she pushed through the hedge. Two hairy black bundles hurtled afterwards, almost tripping her in their eagerness to sniff and investigate Muddle.

'Hi,' she called, 'Glad to see he's friendly.'

'Hi,' answered Daisy. 'Do you normally frequent hedge bottoms or is this a new hobby?'

Grace grinned. 'If you look closely, there's a gate. This is the bottom of our hay field. I usually bring the dogs this way. It saves walking down the road. They're a pair of tinkers on the lead. I didn't realise you lived so near.'

'I don't normally walk this far along but I was lost in my thoughts.'

'What's bothering you?' asked Grace kindly. 'Do you want to walk?'

Daisy hesitated. Grace wouldn't want to listen to her whining. She wouldn't want to be her friend if she thought she was an overprotected wimp who couldn't even go to a church boat race practice. She couldn't let people know how she felt. She'd be a laughing stock. They'd know where her weaknesses lay and would exploit her. She looked away, fighting to banish the destructive monologue. She was anxious not to burden Grace and embarrassed to mention about Friday. But it might help. Grace had only showed her kindness so far.

'Well, maybe for a short while, I ought to go home

soon.'

'Fine.' Grace joined her on the path and called her dogs to follow. Soon all three animals were cavorting joyfully about, apparently delighted to have company.

'Looking forward to the boat race?' began Grace.

'Well, that's rather a problem now...' Daisy faltered.

'Why?' Grace stopped a moment and looked at her.

'There's a family arrangement to visit my aunt,' Daisy explained as they walked on, 'I did ask if I could stay here but my parents aren't keen on my staying home alone yet. Normally Gran would come over but she has a friend staying. That probably sounds ridiculous at my age but it's just how they are!' Daisy laughed to cover her embarrassment.

'Sounds reasonable but I see your dilemma.' Grace surprised Daisy with her response. She was used to people mocking her parents' protectiveness.

'I'll say a quick prayer for you, if you like?' Grace offered. Daisy looked at her quizzically.

'Hey!' Grace exclaimed with a high-five, 'I'll ask if you can stay at mine, if you and your parents would be okay with that?'

'Would your parents mind?' Daisy asked.

'No prob there, we often have friends stopping over.'

'Oh.' Daisy's parents didn't have such a laid-back attitude to friends staying.

'So, if you don't mind helping with a few chores, it'd do me a favour actually. I seem to have this tickle of a cough and there's so much to do this weekend. As usual,

I'm running late with my coursework and I don't want to be ill and miss the race.'

'No.' Daisy wondered what the chores might be.

Grace continued.

'We have sheep, you see, and a couple of goats, hens... we live on a smallholding and are all expected to help out, especially with my dad being away. At the moment, two of my brothers are on holiday as well, so there's more work than ever.'

'That's really kind. I'll ask them. How many brothers do you have?'

'Four.'

Grace stopped suddenly and whipped out her sketchpad and pencil, distracted by a string of hops twining through the hedge. Daisy was going to have to get used to Grace's attention being diverted by her drawing.

It was a great offer though – she liked animals as usually they were easier company than humans. They walked back past the fields, the harvest long since gathered, and parted where they'd met. Daisy now felt more hopeful for the weekend's fun.

Chapter 7 – Delightful Days

Daisy studied the clothes strewn across her bed. Thankfully, her parents after some persuasion were okay with the plan. Mum was feeling much better too so Daisy, looking forward to the weekend now, had set about packing for her stay at Grace's. What to take? She'd be heading back with Grace straight from college on Friday so they'd have time to change and be at the lake for 6 p.m. She thought about what the others had worn on the boating trip and decided on leggings. She tried them on and looked in the mirror. No – her legs looked fat in those. Diet! Ugh, but cutting out treats always made her feel super grumpy. Why couldn't she be more like Grace and just accept the way she was? Jeans? No, too restrictive. What should she take? It would have to be the leggings, perhaps with a tunic top – that would at least cover her thighs! Jeans would be okay for the rest of the time. Tops, underwear, make-up and all that stuff, plus a fleece in case they were out early with the animal chores. Daisy finally had her rucksack packed.

On Friday part way up the lane to Grace's, a gaggle of geese met them, honking as they waddled along.

'Oh no, out again,' sighed Grace, picking up a nearby stick and herding them. 'Come along now, this way!'

Daisy was impressed. She wasn't frightened of geese but wasn't at all sure she could have marshalled them with Grace's success. As they approached the stable door at the back of the farmhouse, Grace's plump mother bustled out in her apron carrying a pan of vegetable scraps.

'Well I never! Have they been up the lane again? Thank you both for bringing them home. Now you're just in time for the jam tarts – fresh from the Aga, they are. Come along in, come along, that's right. Sit you down, Daisy, my dear, delightful to meet you. So glad you can stay.' Mrs Bloom welcomed her, barely stopping for a breath. 'Delightful to have you.'

Daisy felt a giggle rising as she looked around at one of the homeliest rooms she thought she'd ever seen. She felt very much at ease.

Moments later, a batch of warm jam tarts, oozing and fragrant with strawberry jam, appeared on the immense scrubbed table. Daisy's thoughts of strict diets earlier totally melted like the pastry as she tasted the delicious tart. Two of Grace's brothers mysteriously appeared. Reuben, the eldest, was last in and followed by a beautiful dark-skinned girl with deep hazel eyes. He introduced her as Aria. They helped themselves to tarts and sat and chatted until Daisy and Grace set off for the lake, armed with boating gear and looking forward to the café supper afterwards.

It was a fine evening with a gentle breeze and groups of people had gathered around a selection of boats at the water's edge. Daisy felt anxiety creeping up. Why had she agreed to do this?

'You're in this boat with Giorgio and me.' Grace indicated a bright yellow craft. 'Time to board.'

Daisy managed to get in without disaster and relaxed a bit. It felt better being in the same boat as Giorgio and Grace. A sturdy young guy with a rich Yorkshire accent and a whistle started the race with a friendly, 'All the best now to all of you.' They set off.

'That's Pastor Pete,' Grace explained breathlessly as they rowed out.

The six boats set off at a vigorous pace with two clear leaders soon competing to take first place. The boat Daisy was in was tailing near the rear.

'Tactics,' Giorgio had said when she'd pointed this out. Daisy wasn't sure about what these tactics were or how successful they might be, but he had sounded adamant so she didn't feel she could question it. Sure enough, by the time they were halfway across the lake, the early sprint seemed to be taking its toll on the lead boats and the gap between them was closing. Rowing strongly, they managed to take the lead, then Grace suddenly yelped.

'Is it just me with wet feet or have we sprung a leak?' Daisy and Giorgio looked down, dismayed to see the front of their boat beginning to fill with water. They quickly began bailing leaving Grace to row.

It wasn't long before they lost their lead and the boat was still filling up.

'Guys, use my scarf as a plug,' Grace said. She rested one oar and pulled her scarf off.

'Grace!' Daisy yelled as the oar slipped and began to drift away. Grace leaned out to try and catch it, nearly falling out of the boat as she tried to grab it. She lost her scarf as it sank almost immediately.

'Here, I'll take the oars,' Giorgio offered.

By the time they'd finally managed to plug the hole (with a makeshift cork – Grace's art rubber, which she'd discovered in her pocket) and turned, they were the last boat. Grace giggled.

'Well, at least we're still afloat, and it was an old scarf!'

Giorgio laughed and Daisy was impressed by their lightheartedness even though they were losing the race.

With some relief, she saw they were nearing the end. It was definitely becoming choppy and she wasn't sure how long they could rely on their repair work. A mosaic of boats decorated the edge of the lake as they landed their craft. Daisy, Grace and the others hauled the boats out, smoky-coloured mud smudging their hulls as they were pulled to safe port up the grey pebbly shore.

The wind had whipped up now; white flecks crested the blackening water as waves swept in and foamed along the shoreline. Daisy rubbed her arms to ward off the chill creeping over her since she'd stopped rowing. Suddenly, soft warmth blanketed her shoulders and she turned to see Giorgio had given her his jacket. An exquisite joy swept through Daisy. She tried telling herself it was merely a chivalrous act and not to read anything into it, but her senses felt alight as she took in the earthy scent of his cosy fleece. She barely noticed the walk up to the café.

A curl of woodsmoke greeted them as they drew close. At the domed stone oven outside brushing cinders was Giorgio's dad.

'Hey, just a moment.' Giorgio headed toward the oven. Daisy and Grace found a table and began scanning the menu. A slight commotion caused them to look up. It appeared Giorgio was having a heated discussion with his brother.

'He seems really annoyed, Grace. Is that usual?'

Grace shrugged. Daisy looked up anxiously. Giorgio reappeared.

'Hey, sorry guys, my brother's been given an unexpected shift, he has to leave, that's why Dad's manning the pizza oven again. They need my help. Catch you later.'

Daisy fixed her eyes on the menu. Great, she thought – a repeat of last time. Why did he have to go? There she was worrying about letting him and Grace down for the evening for family and now he'd done just that. Was this some kind of excuse to get away from her? He had given her his jacket though. It was all so confusing and she didn't want to spoil the evening.

'Sicilian for me,' Daisy said. Grace chose her pizza and some garlic bread to share again.

'I hope Giorgio's back before it's all gone.' Daisy tried to sound jokey. Grace said nothing.

He didn't reappear. In fact, he was nowhere to be seen when they left. Daisy wondered what to do with his jacket. It would be embarrassing to leave it with his dad since she really didn't know him.

'Keep it for your walk back,' Grace suggested. 'Perhaps you can return it on Sunday if you come to church.'

'Thanks.' Daisy hesitated, not sure whether she'd been invited to church or whether she wanted to go anyway.

It was almost dark by the time they reached the smallholding and Daisy was glad to be shown to her room. As she entered the tiny attic quarters, she breathed in deeply, taking in the delicate fragrance from a generous vase of aromatic dried lavender on the bedside table. Flopping onto the simple pine bed, she felt the freshly pressed pillowcase cool her face. Later as she snuggled into bed, she discovered a hot water bottle with a cosy cover. Within minutes, she fell asleep.

Daisy woke early the next morning. A breeze rippled the gauzy curtains and she noticed sunny splashes patterning the windowsill. A blue sky ran in to meet her as she opened the window wide onto the world. Looking down into the yard below she saw a gate swinging closed and Grace walking into the field with two pails. She could hear her whistling as she went. Wanting to help but feeling unsure, she hesitated at the window. She nearly called to Grace but wary of waking others she decided to check her watch. Only half past six, but she felt refreshed from her deep sleep, so slipping on her jeans and her favourite old turquoise top, she made her way downstairs and out through the yard.

Grace was some way off in the adjacent field but Daisy quickly caught her up by a row of hazel trees where she appeared to be studying the grass.

'What are you looking for? Have you lost something?'

Daisy asked. Surprised in her concentration, Grace jumped.

'Hi! No, I'm looking for field mushrooms; we usually find them around here at this time of year. You can help if you like. Look, here's one!' Grace carefully lifted the mushroom by its stalk and turned it over so Daisy could see the velvety black underside.

'Are you sure?' questioned Daisy, being aware some weren't safe to eat.

'Sure,' confirmed Grace. 'We have them every year!'

Daisy helped gather the fungi and placed them in the paper-lined basket.

'To be honest, it's great to have some help,' Grace told Daisy as they carried on with the chores. 'There's always so much to do around here and Mum works hard when Dad's away. I mean, we're kind of used to helping out as a family but it's totally not at the top of my fun list.'

'What's it like with your dad being away so much?'

'I've kind of grown up with it so I don't know much different. In fact, it throws a bit of a curveball when he's home. It's great to see him of course, but everything kind of revolves around him while he's here. We all want to catch up and hear what he's been up to – the bits he can tell us, that is. Then he's gone and everything is a bit flat for a while.'

'Yeah, I guess it's a bit weird. I sometimes wish I had a bit more space from my parents but I s'pose it would be odd if one of them was away a lot.'

Sauntering back to the house, they reached the farm

gate and smelled bacon. Mrs Bloom was delighted with the find and immediately added the mushrooms to a pan sizzling with foaming butter.

'I'm really hungry,' Grace said, sitting down to a huge plateful.

Daisy tucked in. She'd decided to be more relaxed about food, like Grace. After all, with all this boating, she was doing plenty of exercise now. She thoroughly enjoyed the breakfast feast, thinking the taste of the freshly gathered mushrooms was the best.

Saturday flew by in a whirl of animal-related activities which Daisy revelled in; kitchen scraps to the hens, ducks and geese, collecting eggs, walking the dogs and picking late beans from the vegetable garden. Standing for a moment leaning on the farm gate, she spotted the cat enjoying creamy cool milk in a spot of shade. Life seemed peaceful and contented here despite the busy farm.

In the afternoon, the girls were free to please themselves and decided to reward their hard work by going down to the café for another ice.

'I'll take Giorgio's jacket.' Daisy didn't see him but she enjoyed a large raspberry sorbet and chatting with Grace.

'Would you like to come to our church, Willows, tomorrow? It starts at 10 a.m. and it's, well, not too formal – no obligation.' Grace asked as they were about to leave.

Daisy hesitated; she was keen to see Giorgio and

she had his coat to return, but something told her that these were not the best motives. Also, she was not at all sure she liked church. Her experiences as a child there had usually resulted in her feeling guilty and not good enough. However, Grace's comments about informality intrigued her and of course she might see Giorgio.

'Okay, I guess.'

Later that night, tired though she was from all the fresh air, Daisy didn't find it easy to sleep. Going round and round in her mind was her decision to go to church. Butterflies dipped and dived in her stomach, and she felt like rushing into Grace's room to say she'd changed her mind. Perhaps she could say she was ill in the morning? No, the idea of lying to her friend didn't sit well with her, and besides, she wanted to see Giorgio even if he did keep disappearing half the time. She'd just have to go despite her wobbly feelings.

Chapter 8 – Divine Days

'These are delicious!' Daisy licked her lips and took another bite of the cinnamon pancakes made with the eggs they'd collected yesterday. They headed off to church after breakfast. It looked like a revamped old warehouse, Daisy thought, as they approached the modern glass doors. Inside it was warm and the scent of good coffee wafted across the comfortable foyer. This was quite unlike her previous experiences of cold, austere and musty-smelling buildings. Fresh flowers adorned tables by a door leading through to the main body of the church, which was light and airy with cushion-clad chairs dotted around. A low semi-circular platform graced the area in front of the chairs and on it sat a drum kit, several guitars, a saxophone and a keyboard. Daisy struggled to take in all these differences as people began to fill up the chairs.

'Let's sit near the front.' Grace indicated a row. 'We'll hear the music better.'

Daisy felt uncomfortable being near the front but didn't like to say as this was her first visit. Then Giorgio appeared and sat next to her, which took away all thoughts of moving instantly. She smiled and handed him his jacket.

'Hey, thanks for remembering.'

'A warm welcome to you all,' Pastor Pete began.

Daisy listened with interest to the readings, noticing one was given by a member of the congregation. The readings sounded different from those she was vaguely familiar with from her childhood, somehow less... formal, yes, just as Grace had said. The music was wonderful and the hymns, or songs really, she thought were lovely. Some of the words brought tears to her eyes but desperate not to be emotional in front of people, she dug her fingernails into her palms and tried to concentrate on the woodgrain in the floor.

The sermon actually was more of a talk and Daisy was amazed at the gentle message given. It talked of a God, with whom she was definitely not familiar, who thought she was wonderful and cared for her. She found herself feeling drawn to know more about Him. The service was quite short too. Even Dad would have liked it, she thought. "A good sermon's always a short sermon." She recalled his stock phrase whenever he had to attend church for "hatches, matches and despatches" as he called them.

'Let's find a drink,' Grace suggested afterwards, and Giorgio led the way to a kind of atrium decorated with lush green plants and coffee tables.

Armchairs and sofas surrounded a bar serving lattes, cappuccinos and healthy snacks. Daisy was amazed. This was unlike any other church she'd ever visited. She liked it. Smiling inside and out, she relaxed into one of the squishy armchairs and picked up a menu.

'Please let me get these,' Daisy said when they'd all decided. She headed to the bar.

'What's through there?' she queried, noticing a

doorway on her way back.

'Hey, that's the bookshop,' said Giorgio. 'We can take a look after we've finished our drinks if you like.'

Daisy nodded.

Half an hour later, they stood in a well-stocked shop with free lending library. She picked up one or two books, including a novel that she decided to buy. At the pay desk she saw a computer with downloads available and noticed with delight there was some harp music. On an impulse, she downloaded a few tracks. Before all heading off to church, the Blooms had eaten a light buffet-style lunch, which everyone had helped put together.

Later, preparations began for a sumptuous tea including "scrumbles" made with home-grown lavender, which were a kind of cross between crumble and scones with a few scented lavender seeds sprinkled into the mixture; fragrant and utterly delicious. Mrs Bloom had also baked an enormous bramble and apple pie.

'Using the last of the late summer blackberries, and there's lashings of cream or custard, or both!' she invited.

There was some cooked fruit left over and after loading the dishwasher, Grace and Daisy took it to the barn freezer. Peering into its roomy depths, Daisy oohed at the trays of juicy blackcurrants, strings of luscious redcurrants and frozen apple rings.

'Are these all from your garden?' she asked, impressed by the array of produce.

Grace nodded. 'The pantry shelves are lined with homemade jams too; gooseberry, raspberry, strawberry.

Mum loves to make good use of everything.' Daisy was reminded of cooking with her grandma.

After tea and expressing her appreciation for such a fabulous weekend, Daisy made her way home.

Her family weren't yet back so she thought she'd listen to the new harp tracks. Glancing at the list of artists, Daisy looked again and saw Giorgio's name alongside one track. Amazing. She forwarded to his track and listened with wonder as the lilting chords filled the room. The track seemed somehow familiar and she soon recognised it as the one she'd heard while listening outside the music room at Waterside. Could this really be Giorgio playing? How wonderful to have your own music recorded! Resolving to ask Grace about it tomorrow, she shut her eyes and allowed herself to be absorbed in the music.

The instrumental track was beautiful. Daisy drifted into a daydream as the music flowed into her room. She played it again and again. Wow, he's an amazing harpist, she thought, I wonder why I've never seen him in music classes? She hoped she would soon hear him in person. Feeling inspired, Daisy took out her own harp and practised the recent piece she'd been given at college to play. Surprisingly, she found she managed the piece without error. She looked forward to her next lesson. Perhaps she could ask her harp teacher about Giorgio? Barks from Muddle heralded the return of the rest of the family and Daisy felt it would help if she offered to make supper as her mum would be tired after the long journey. Mum's weary face lit up at this unexpected proposal and

Daisy set about preparing the meal. Humming Giorgio's track as she stirred the spicy tomato sauce for their pasta, Daisy found herself smiling, a smile that seemed to rise from her heart.

'You're very cheerful this evening,' stated Dad, looking at her quizzically. 'It seems it did you good to stay with that new friend of yours.' Daisy grinned inwardly knowing it wasn't just Grace's friendship that was the reason for her happiness.

After supper, Daisy went up to her room, put on Giorgio's track again and pulled out her phone to message Jonno. "Hi, hope you're okay and can message soon. That new friend I mentioned, her name's Grace, she invited me to stay so I could go to the event. I had an amazing time – great food. You'd like her. She's kind, fun and really into art. She lives on a kind of smallholding with escaping geese and all sorts – you'd love it. It was pretty good later too. We went to the lake with Giorgio – yes, I can hear you say, but no, it's not like that! Well, not yet! I have to admit to a few hopes there though! Grace goes to church so I went with her on Sunday – yes, really. It was totally different, kind of cool. Giorgio was there too and wait for this – he plays the harp! He's even recorded a few tracks. I'm loving his music. Message me! Love Daze!"

She played the track through again, drifting back into her dreamy landscape, imagining joining Giorgio to play. With these delightful thoughts, she fell asleep.

Chapter 9 – Dramatic Days

Daisy, just about to set off for college early the next morning, was busy gathering harp scores for her music case when Dad appeared.

'I wish I could take my own harp to school.' Daisy looked at him optimistically.

'It's too difficult to transport. Just be glad you can borrow one from the college's collection. Mum's car's too small to fit it into even when you can borrow it, and all being well for Mum, that won't be for much longer.'

'Couldn't I borrow yours?'

'Out of the question, it'd be far too expensive to insure you at your age, but if you can find a holiday job over Christmas perhaps, next year you'll be able to afford a larger old car, then you could take it.'

'Fat chance round here.'

'Daisy.' Dad gave her one of his "enough" looks.

She slid out, glad she had her first two lessons free for study time and could go directly to the music rooms.

At school as she reached the corridor, she glimpsed Giorgio opening the door to the far music room. Her heart leapt and she opened her mouth to call him to see if they could practice together, then abruptly shut it as a sturdy good-looking guy emerged and embraced Giorgio, kissing him delicately on both cheeks before heading towards the door. Daisy turned and fled.

Searing waves of jealousy and confusion coursed

through her. She felt hot and cold at the same time. Was Giorgio gay? No! It was okay for Jonno to be gay but not Giorgio, please. She hadn't misread him, surely? Maybe he was bi and that was why he was so evasive. Maybe he couldn't decide, or perhaps he just liked her as a friend but didn't want to be too close. Why couldn't he just say? Anger raged within her and she felt tempted to kick the nearest door or scream. Finally, reason took hold. You cannot have a tantrum, you're not a toddler, a voice in her head said, but it didn't help the way she felt. Too sick at heart to think about harp practice and at a loss to cope with her feelings, she drew them tightly inside and walked out into the fresh air.

She walked towards the library, not knowing where else to go. She decided to try and see if she could find a good fiction book. At least fictional characters can't hurt me, she thought.

On her way, she spotted Lucy having what appeared to be a violent argument with her entourage. She wondered what was going on. Although Daisy disliked Lucy following her last encounter, she somehow felt compelled to walk closer. What do you think you're doing? A voice squealed in her head. This will only upset you more. Walk away!

Daisy thought the voice had a good point and began to divert just as Lucy tore across her path, head low, tears streaming down her face. Daisy stopped in her tracks, feeling alarmed. Lucy's usual squad sauntered by, ignoring her but sniggering together.

One of them remarked loudly, 'Well, it's her own fault!'

'What do you think she'll do now?'

'Who cares?'

Despite Lucy's previous treatment of her, Daisy felt a stab of compassion. She knew so well how it felt to be jeered at and abandoned by so-called friends. She considered following Lucy to ask if she could help. She was fearful of a venomous response, then decided she'd be courageous.

'Lucy?' Daisy called with concern, running closer. Lucy kept ahead so Daisy, thinking she might not have heard, called again.

'Naff off!' Lucy yelled, gesturing obscenely. Daisy stopped, her face flaring hot with embarrassment and shame. Why had she thought Lucy would want anything to do with her, even if she was trying to help? Feeling sad, drained and wishing she wasn't so emo, Daisy stopped at the coffee machine outside the library door and bought herself a mocha. Sipping the sweet hot drink, she tried to comfort herself with soothing suggestions. Life could still be good even if Giorgio did have a boyfriend and Lucy hated her. She still felt totally miserable though.

Unable to bear anyone witnessing the hot tears that threatened, she forced herself to leave her drink and walk up to the library desk. Her pride wouldn't allow her to weep there. Asking the librarian for information she already knew about closing times allowed Daisy the chance to restrain her emotions. Noticing Grace poring over something on her laptop, Daisy slid onto the bench alongside her.

'Hi,' whispered Grace, 'I'm desperate to finish this piece of work. There's a gig at church tonight, Giorgio's playing. I really want to go but I was late handing in the last assignment and this one's due tomorrow. I can't believe it. I triple-checked the date but somehow I still muddled it. I can't go if I don't get it done!'

'No worries, I'll leave you in peace,' Daisy said.

'Thanks,' whispered Grace, concentrating. 'Hey, join me for the gig if you like? You can stay over at ours if it helps?'

Daisy froze.

'Er, no thanks, I need to, er, head off,' she stammered, quickly moving away. Grace had probably seen the look in her eyes and pitied her. Daisy hurried out.

It was ironic, she thought, trying to ignore another pang of rejection. How could she say "no worries" to people all the time when she barely ever stopped worrying? Daisy couldn't settle herself to read either now. Frustration erupted. She wanted to see and hear Giorgio play and enjoy herself at a musical evening with friends, but she had to suppress any feelings of anger and envy that would resurface. She would probably lose it if she set eyes on him so soon after seeing him with... that boy. Not to mention the excruciating humiliation of being invited just because Grace felt sorry for her.

Daisy fretted over this conflict and felt guilty at being so off-hand with Grace, who certainly didn't deserve to be treated like that. She'd catastprohised, she reflected. They'd talked about that in the therapy class she and Jonno had attended. Finally, the bell for lessons rang. Daisy considered ducking out but she had a music exam the following week so she made herself concentrate on the tasks for the day.

After college, it was raining as she walked towards the exit. Daisy heard Grace calling her from the pond area by the refectory. Fearing she'd be persuaded to go to the gig and not wanting to get soaked (she'd forgotten her waterproof), Daisy waved a hand and carried on towards home.

'Daisy!' repeated Grace. The urgency in Grace's tone at once irritated Daisy and concerned her. Turning round, she saw Grace was with Lucy, who seemed seriously agitated. Grace beckoned her over to the bike shed. Daisy hesitated. Well, she could always leave if she wanted to. She went across towards her friend.

'Lucy needs some help...' Grace began as Daisy approached. Indignation now bubbled furiously within Daisy, threatening to launch a vitriolic refusal as she thought of Lucy's earlier rebuff and the incident in the corridor during her first week at college. But as she opened her mouth, she caught a beseeching gleam in Grace's eyes.

Daisy's compassion returned and she found herself asking instead, 'What's wrong?'

'Nothing you can help with,' spat Lucy.

Daisy made to leave but a streak of lightning flashed

across the sky followed by a crack of thunder, which made them all jump.

'Lucy.' Grace placed a calming hand on her shoulder. 'You can probably use some extra friends right now.'

'Oh!' Lucy burst out. 'I'm so scared. I'm in so much trouble. I've been so stupid.'

Daisy found it really difficult to show physical affection to people she didn't know well ever since the therapy group where hugs had been enforced. She felt even less inclined to hug someone who'd belittled her. She dug in her bag and offered Lucy a tissue.

'I thought he really cared,' Lucy wailed, dabbing her eyes, 'I really thought people would think I mattered if someone cared about me. I should've realised. Now he's gone off with someone else, put some totally embarrassing crap about me on social media – jerk – a kind of rating system! Worst thing though, I am left with... I can't bear to think about it, and my so-called friends, well... you heard them.'

Lucy sank to the floor, cradled her head in her hands and cried piteously.

The storm continued. Massive droplets of rain splashed into the bike shed forming puddles of water. Daisy was worried these would reach the already sodden Lucy. She felt really upset for her and wondered what was wrong. She didn't know how she could help. 'Lucy,' Grace, asked gently, 'what are you frightened about?'

'I think I may be pregnant,' Lucy began, 'and what's worse, I think I may have some diseases. This guy... he told me he wasn't keen on, well, using protection. I didn't think... he was, well, you know "popular" with girls, and then I found out he was and was into other stuff too. I'll spare you the details!'

'Oh, Lucy,' Grace spoke, her voice gentle, 'I'm sure there's something we can do to help, I'm just not sure what.' The storm seemed to be moving on.

'Well,' began Daisy, 'I had a friend at my last school who had a kind of similar problem. I could...'

'As if you'd know anything.' Lucy turned away. Daisy made to leave but Grace held up her hand.

'Wait! Lucy, stop sneering, please. If Daisy knows how to help, let her.'

Daisy admired Grace. She felt scared of Lucy herself and would never dare say such a thing. Lucy looked at Daisy with a glimmer of hope in her eyes.

'Really? Can you help?' Her voice sounded small and quite unlike the caustic tone Daisy had so often heard.

'Well, my friend, erm, he needed some, er, health checks. There is help. You'd need an appointment but maybe, if you like, if it's okay with Grace, we can come with you,' Daisy suggested, looking hopefully at Grace.

'Great plan, and maybe you can help Lucy find information about all this?' said Grace.

'I can if you like?' Daisy offered, amazed to hear Grace speak like this. She'd expected the sort of judgemental attitude she'd sometimes heard back in Sunday School when there was gossip about someone who was apparently not running a straight course.

'Why don't you come to the gig at church tonight?' Grace suggested, 'It might take your mind off things a bit. How about you, Daisy?'

Daisy thought her jealousy seemed petty now and that perhaps it would be a way to offer some friendship to Lucy.

'Er, yes, I think I can go after all.'

Lucy said thanks but that she didn't feel up to being in company at the moment.

'Okay,' said Grace, 'but what about this health check? Let's phone about the appointment then we all know what time we need to be free.'

The rain had stopped by the time they'd sorted Lucy's appointment so they headed out.

'How do you know all that stuff?' Grace asked when they'd left Lucy.

'A friend of mine at my last school, Jonno, he had some concerns. He asked me to go with him to get some info. I kind of knew from that.'

Daisy thought back to the day Jonno had come to find her in the library and had said, 'Daze, I need you to help me out.' She'd agreed of course, and he'd gone on to say, 'Well, you were ace helping me to tell my parents, but now, well, I've kind of met someone. Well, you know I was telling you about that guy at Dance? Anyway, things may be, er, developing, and I need to get some info so we can be safe.' Daisy explained this to Grace.

'So, I went along with him to the sexual health clinic. We read through all the leaflets while he waited for his appointment with an adviser. It was a real eye-opener, I can tell you. I mean, I know they say stuff at school in those totally embarrassing "facts of life" classes and parents mutter about stuff, but honestly, I had no idea about, well, the variety of... issues, that can arise for... various reasons... resulting from activities that... well, let's not go there. Just to say I know for sure there's help available for Lucy.'

Grace stood open-mouthed for a moment.

'Well, you're amazing to have helped Lucy like that, especially when she'd been less than kind to you.'

'I think you're pretty cool yourself. I mean, you are always friendly to people even when you know they can be, well, to be honest, literally sus.'

'I guess I learnt this when I needed a second chance.'

'Go on. I mean, if you don't mind saying. It's totally okay if not.'

'So the thing is, I... oh, this is so embarrassing. Well, I had this crush on one of my teachers at my last school and, well, let's just say I made a total idiot of myself.' Grace cringed. Daisy looked at her kindly, so she continued.

'I used to wait for him to come out of class and offer to carry books for him. I completely adored him. Then one day there was just me and him in the classroom at the end of the day and I stood so close I sort of brushed against him. That was when he looked at me. I thought he wanted to kiss me so, can you believe it, I moved closer. Anyway, he then gave me a gentle chat on "inappropriateness". I felt so humiliated, you can't imagine. He was super cool about it though, so somehow I was able to go on in his class without anyone else finding out. I mean, he could have had me expelled.' Grace hesitated. 'I, er, I never told anyone, but I know you won't say anything.'

Daisy felt a warm glow. It was great to be trusted. 'Of course not. I sort of felt the same about my geography master a year or so ago.' She looked up at Grace. They both laughed and it felt like a "friends forever" laugh. They fist-bumped then both headed back home.

Chapter 10 – Daunting Days

Daisy messaged Grace when she arrived home to check the time of the gig and they made arrangements to meet at the church at 7.30 p.m. Grace also said Lucy had asked her to let Daisy know they were going to an appointment the next day. Grace asked if Daisy would pray that all would go well. Daisy was surprised and not really sure about praying but before getting ready, she sat on the edge of her bed and tried to say what she remembered from Sunday School prayers. Somehow though it didn't seem enough. What would she say if God were here in front of her, or if say she could message Him?

'God,' she faltered, 'this probably isn't the right way to talk to you but I don't know what else to say so... I'm worried for my friend, Lucy. I don't know why I call her a friend because, as you already know, just this morning I really didn't like her. In fact, I thought I hated her because she'd taunted me. You were probably not very happy about those feelings but I have to be honest because we both know they were there. I often have feelings I don't like about things, feelings that, well, make me think really crappy – sorry, I mean horrid – things about others. You know this, of course. I can't hide anything from you, but all this "feelings" stuff really screws me up,' she sighed.

'Please help me out here. Why am I talking about my feelings when I'm supposed to be praying for Lucy? Why am I asking you that? Sorry. Now I'll try and concentrate.

So Lucy, you know about her troubles, God, and the way Grace is helping her. I would like to be more helpful to her too but I'm frightened. Please will you give her all the help she needs in whatever way you know is best? As honestly, it feels beyond me. Thank you. Amen.' Daisy felt lighter after this informal prayer than she'd ever felt after the prayers she had read at her childhood church. Perhaps, she thought, God would help her not to feel jealous at the gig that night.

It was soon 7.30 p.m. and Daisy stood waiting at the church door. Her heart leapt as she saw Giorgio but then sank as he was followed closely by That Boy. Daisy forced a smile.

'Hey, hi,' called Giorgio, 'meet my cousin, Stefano, he's accompanying me tonight, he has an amazing voice.' Cousin? Stefano leaned and kissed her on both cheeks. Daisy smiled – of course, an Italian greeting!

'Pleased to meet you,' she said with genuine feeling, 'I very much look forward to hearing you both.' Inwardly she jumped with glee. A cousin! Why had she made assumptions and jumped to conclusions? She could have saved herself all that heartache.

Grace arrived, catching her breath. 'Only just finished that wretched essay,' she gasped. 'Come on, let's grab some seats.'

The performance was amazing and, incredibly, there was a piece that Stefano played on the jazz harp. Daisy was mesmerised.

'If you like this music,' the Pastor said to the congregation, 'then you can download the album "Praise Him on the Harp" from our bookshop.' Daisy did a double-take. That was the album she owned! She'd been so obsessed with listening to Giorgio's track she hadn't even realised there was a jazz harp track. She must put it on again!

Next followed a short piece from the Bible. The reading was from Isaiah 65 about God's promises for the future, and Verse 24 struck her: "Before they call, I will answer. While they are still speaking, I will hear." Daisy's heart warmed as she remembered her unspoken question to God about her jealousy. She also felt sure in her spirit that all would be well for Lucy. The prayer concluding the evening was just a few words of thanks for God's care. Daisy liked that.

Just as she and Grace were about to leave, Giorgio approached them. He looked rather awkwardly at Grace, who shrugged her shoulders and moved over to look at the bookstall.

'Hey Daisy,' stammered Giorgio shyly. 'I was wondering – no pressure, of course – but I heard that you play the harp too. Would you like to practise with me sometime?'

'Yes!' Daisy said delightedly, then wondered to her horror what she'd just agreed to. She felt in no way adequate to match his heart-melting harmonies.

'Great,' continued Giorgio, 'how about tomorrow at two in the first music room? It's free then if you are.'

Daisy thought about backtracking. She must be mad, she thought. How would she ever equal him? Yet she found herself agreeing.

Grace returned and they walked together towards the door, with Grace giving her a knowing smile.

'What?' Daisy asked, blushing.

Chapter 11 – Days of Determination

Daisy met Giorgio in the music room. Her harp was there. Dad had surprised her by dropping it off earlier. Daisy felt so nervous that she spilt the contents of her music case across the floor as she tried to take out the sheets of harp music. Giorgio picked them up for her before she had a chance, then he pulled a chair across for her and sat next to her with his harp positioned ready. Daisy took her seat and placed her music on the stand.

'I never thought to ask what we'd play,' she said shyly, 'I only have a few pieces with me.'

'Hey, let's share,' Giorgio suggested.

As they bent their heads over the music together, Daisy was aware of his earthy scent and had difficulty concentrating on what he was saying. They began to play the music. At first, Daisy struggled to keep up, but Giorgio altered the pace to suit her and soon she was lost in the beauty of the music. It'd been a long time since she'd enjoyed playing her harp so much. After a while, they stopped.

'Do you take music? I never see you in class,' Daisy asked.

'No, I have to work some hours at the café so I just take business and accounts. I'd love to do music but one day I'd like to run a music café, so I really need to get the business know-how. It's all changing from how Dad did things and if we don't change with the times, there'll be no café to run.'

He didn't seem to want to say any more so they began to play again. He didn't seem to mind not taking music but he clearly loved it. She wondered how he could be so cool about not doing it. It was a pretty big sacrifice he was making there but hey, it would be amazing to have a music café. Maybe people could come for lessons, even little ones; she'd love to do that. Maybe have a "Musical Moments" session for toddlers where parents and carers could come and have coffee and ices too... What was she thinking? She hardly knew Giorgio yet was dreaming about working with him already!

They'd been in the music room for almost two hours when the caretaker knocked on the door and announced he was locking up. They hadn't noticed the time race by and she was meant to meet Grace and Lucy in a few minutes. As they left, Giorgio slowed.

'Hey...' He hesitated and cleared his throat. 'I... I was wondering if, well, if you'd like to come to supper later?' Daisy felt thrilled and delved into her shoulder bag for her phone to hide her elation.

'I'll need to check, but that sounds great, thanks,' she said, texting as she spoke. Her family preferred to have more notice usually, but to Daisy's joy, tonight her Mum had prepared salad and said it could go in the fridge and that it would be fine so long as she was back by 10 p.m. Daisy turned to Giorgio and nodded.

Daisy, Lucy and Grace sat in the waiting room of the

clinic. It was painted a bleak grey and there were no pictures on the walls. All they could hear was the tap-tap of the receptionist's keyboard. Lucy was flicking randomly through the magazines, clearly not reading anything. Daisy watched her pale face and anxious eyes. The tannoy sounded announcing her name and Lucy jumped. Grace put her hand on Lucy's and gave it a squeeze.

'We'll be here and praying for you,' Grace assured her. Lucy shot her a grateful glance. Grace took out a notebook and began to draw.

'Your drawings are brilliant but what exactly is that?' Daisy looked closely at the picture of two hands forming a heart shape with an L in the centre.

'It's what I call a prayer picture. When my grandfather had a sudden stroke, the hospital chaplain gave me a Celtic prayer book with beautiful illustrations that suggested this way of praying. I find it really useful when I feel overwhelmed.'

Daisy nodded. 'I can understand how that could help. I guess I use music in that kind of a way, sort of.'

'Talking of music, I heard you and Giorgio are practising together. Is that all about the music?' Grace asked, arching her eyebrows.

Daisy blushed and grinned.

'What about you?' she countered. 'Anyone special in your life?'

'Last year there was but we had a grim break, he behaved like a complete... well, I don't want to go into that, and now the only guy I'm interested in is away at university. As far as I can tell, he's not even tuned into my existence. But hey, as Giorgio would say, I'm a patient woman and it's not long 'til Christmas. He'll be home for the holidays hopefully so who knows?'

'Well...' said Daisy, but stopped as Lucy appeared rubbing her tear-streaked cheeks. Her head was down.

'Please, let's go,' she muttered.

They walked through the park. As they reached the riverbank, Lucy sat down on a bench and the others joined her. They were all quiet for some time. It grew colder and Daisy pulled on her hoodie.

Lucy spoke.

'I'm not pregnant, which is good. The other business is more complicated. I've had all the tests but I have to wait until next week for results, and for two of the tests I have to come back and have them re-done. It'll be months before I know for sure.' Lucy began to beat her fists on her knees. 'Why did I do it? I'm so scared.'

Grace spoke softly. 'Don't be so hard on yourself. We all do things we wish we hadn't. Sometimes it takes some of us ages before we realise it just isn't the best for us.'

'Thanks.' Lucy shivered. 'I just don't know how I'm going to get through all this.'

'You will.' Grace put her arm around Lucy's shoulders. 'God's gracious, and we're here for you. You will.'

'I'm seriously cold.' Lucy wrapped her arms around herself. 'I have to go home now anyway. I'm meant to do tea Tuesdays as Mum works late and there's just the two of us. You've been really kind. It's helped me so much. I work as a waitress Wednesday and Friday evenings and at the weekend. If either of you are free Thursday though, just to chat? There's no-one else I can really talk to.'

Daisy could hardly believe Lucy was considering talking to her now. She still felt nervous of her but guessed it must be hard with just her and her mum. She herself had found it difficult taking on some of Mum's tasks when her eyes had been bad. She supposed Lucy had extra tasks all the time.

'What time?' Daisy asked. 'Only I have to collect Rosie that day. Mum's going for her final eye check.'

'I'm free all Thursday evening.' Grace agreed to meet Lucy after college.

'I still think it would be good if you let your mum know, but I understand that would be hard.'

'I know, but I keep hoping that maybe there's no need.'

'I hope so too but I'm sure she'd want to support you.'

'I'll think about it. I think she might just get really angry.'

'Well, I'll pray for you. See you Thursday.'

On the way home, they passed a book and stationery shop.

'Perhaps we could buy a journal for Lucy. Do you think she'd like that?' Daisy asked.

Grace nodded. 'I don't have any money though.'

'No worries, I do. Dad gave me some to thank me for helping out so much while Mum's eyes were bad.' Daisy dug in her bag for her purse.

Together they chose a beautiful journal embroidered with pink and gold Japanese anemones on a white background. There was a coffee bar in the shop so they decided to stop for a drink while Grace wrote an encouraging scripture in it for Lucy. She illustrated it with one of her amazing sketches.

'You're a brilliant artist, Grace.'

Grace raised one eyebrow in modesty before going back to her drawing.

Daisy looked at the tiny Bible Grace was using. She was struck by the way how in Psalms it seemed that David (who it said wrote them) talked to God. "Do not be far from me, for trouble is near." Then later, David was able to say, "God is our refuge and strength, an ever present help in trouble." She mentioned this to Grace.

'Well,' Grace replied, 'I wonder sometimes if God thinks I'm slightly offhand with him, chatting in this way. I was taught to know him as "Abba Father" though, which means "Daddy", so why would he want formal distant prayers?'

Daisy said nothing but considered this while Grace slipped the old pocket Bible into a bag with the journal along with a bookmark.

'Right, ready?' Grace glanced at her watch. 'Nearly five-thirty already, I'd better dash. I'm supposed to be sorting the animals this evening. See you tomorrow?'

Daisy nodded and gathered her things. She was in a hurry too. It was time for her to go to the café. There was no time to change now. She hoped she looked okay.

When she arrived at the café, Giorgio was waiting outside.

'Hey, hi, come on in.' He led Daisy around to the side entrance.

'Mama, Papa, questo es Daisy.'

'Yahsu! Hello!' His mum greeted her as they stepped into a homely kitchen. The lemon-coloured walls and bright potted geraniums dotted around the sills gave a Mediterranean feel. Giorgio's dad was busy at the range cooker and an appetising aroma of garlic filled the room. He turned as Daisy came in.

'Buongiorno.' Giorgio's dad, a great bear of a man, welcomed her with a warm hug and a kiss on both cheeks, echoing the enthusiasm of his wife.

'You are so welcome,' his mum continued, 'we love to meet Giorgio's friends. I hope you enjoy spaghetti? Giuseppe is just making the sauce.'

Daisy nodded. She wanted to ask if she could help in any way but felt shy, then she noticed Giorgio inviting her to join him. She followed him through arched French windows onto a raised terrace, bathed in the last rays of sunlight. Petunias still overflowed in tubs along the edges and a late honeysuckle clambered up a trellis and spilled into the neighbour's garden, decanting a share of its honeyed fragrance.

'This is gorgeous, I love the scent of the honeysuckle.'

Giorgio grinned and began laying the table so she offered to give him a hand. Soon they were joined by Giorgio's older brother, Yannis.

'Salve! Salve!' he boomed.

Daisy didn't know the meaning of all these greeting words but was confident from their manner that Giorgio's family were pleased to see her. Her heart fluttered with pleasure. She felt at ease and was soon chatting to Yannis, who she learnt was setting up a boat renting business on the lake. A brief prayer of thanks was offered by Giorgio's dad and the meal began.

'This food's super good,' Daisy said.

'The sauce is made with tomatoes we grow and bottle,' said Rosa.

'In Italy,' Giuseppe explained, 'it is known as "sugo". We add our garlic and herbs.' He indicated the pots just outside the door and a string of bulbs hanging by the window. 'We used to make it in our restaurant in Amorgos, Greece.' Daisy noticed a sadness creep into his eyes.

'I loved that place,' he continued, 'we both did. It's where I met Rosa.' He gave a cheeky grin. 'But,' the sadness to his voice returned, 'we had to leave our beautiful island because of the Greek economy. Hey, let's not talk of sad things though. We have a great café now.'

No wonder Giorgio did business instead of music, Daisy thought.

He poured some wine and offered a glass to Daisy. She wasn't used to drinking alcohol. She wondered whether she should accept. If she didn't, they might think she was being rude or judgemental, but if she did, what if it made her do something daft or get giggly?

'Wine with meals is usual in Italy and Greece,' said Giorgio, seeing her hesitation.

'A small amount, please,' Daisy said. She poured water too as she saw the others had done then gladly accepted when offered a refill. She was rewarded with a gleeful grin from Giorgio's parents.

'It is from our friend's vineyard,' Rosa explained, pouring herself a second glass.

Later, thick creamy yoghurt was served with honey.

'It's from our bees,' Rosa announced proudly, indicating the honey. 'We keep them just a short distance from the café in the field of the farmer next door.'

'Delicious!' Daisy said after savouring the last spoonful.

When they'd helped clear away, Giorgio suggested a walk by the lake. Daisy glanced at her watch; she had half an hour. They made their way down. The evening was warm so they sat on the jetty, took off their socks and shoes and nudged their toes into the soft sand at the edge of the pebbles.

Giorgio put his hand on the jetty. Daisy noticed it was quite near hers and longed to move her fingers so they touched. Giorgio picked up a stray pebble from the jetty and skimmed it, then he jumped down to pick up a few more. Disappointment coursed through Daisy but she decided to join him, and for quite a while they competed, Daisy's pebbles giving Giorgio's a fair challenge. Laughing, they jumped back on the jetty, and this time he moved his hand to cover hers. Tiny shivers of delight ran through her as his fingers closed over hers. He touched her cheek gently so she turned to look at him. He held her gaze with his chocolate eyes.

'You're beautiful, Daisy.'

Daisy blushed. She wanted to tell him how wonderful she thought he was but no words would come.

The sun dipped beneath the horizon and Daisy realised she'd soon need to make her way home. She longed for him to take her in his arms but he jumped up and grabbed his shoes.

'Hey, I'll walk you home.' He headed down the jetty.

'Oh, no worries, I'll be fine.' Daisy felt confused.

'No, I must.'

They walked in silence. Daisy didn't know what to say.

'Hey, did you enjoy the music practice?' he asked when they reached her gate.

'Yes, I did.'

'Would you like to make it regular?'

Daisy nodded, hopeful he might kiss her goodbye. He waved instead and was gone.

She went into the house calling 'hi!' then crept quickly upstairs, eager to retreat to her room, relive the memories of the evening, and try to work out the enigmatic Giorgio.

Later while she dozed in bed, she played the music she'd downloaded. This time, instead of just repeating Giorgio's track, she let it play on and was delighted to hear the jazz harp being played. I wish I could try that, she thought – she just loved the sound. Perhaps she could ask Mrs Stringer.

Chapter 12 – Disconcerting Days

Thursday soon arrived. 'I said I'd go around the lake later with Lucy. Join us. I know you may be busy but if you can,' Grace said as they went off to their classes. Daisy felt a spike of jealousy. Grace seemed to be spending loads of time with Lucy lately. You know she's only being supportive so don't go there! She warned herself. Later, Daisy found she was free so she decided to join them. Lucy was running and Daisy could see she was really upset when she and Grace arrived.

'My mum found out!' Lucy blurted. 'My so-called friends were gossiping about me and one of their mothers asked my mother. Complete nightmare. My mother thinks I have all sorts of dreadful diseases and keeps cleaning up after me. She's so uptight, she's had to make an appointment to see the doctor. I feel really guilty. I never even thought my actions might affect other people.' Breaking into sobs again, she hid her face and crouched down by the lakeside. Grace put an arm around her and waited until her weeping had subsided.

'God can bring good even out of circumstances that seem pretty horrendous. One day at a time. I know it's cliché but just try to think about the rest of today for now. This lake's beautiful. Let's see if we can make it all around before sunset.'

They set off and Grace worked hard to keep Lucy's spirits up, chatting about a new club at college and encouraging Lucy to join. Daisy backed her up. She wanted to help but it felt exhausting giving out all this emotional support.

Grace was so good at this stuff.

'I don't know. What use would I be?' Lucy kicked at the edge of the grass.

'You're smart, Lucy. It's a debating club, you'd be great.'

Daisy nodded as Grace urged Lucy to reconsider. By the time they'd completed the lake walk, she'd agreed to help with the organisation at least.

'It'll be something to concentrate on while I wait to hear if I'm okay... or not,' Lucy muttered. Grace gave her the journal and they parted.

Grace and Daisy carried on together as Daisy was going over to Grace's to help her finish some long overdue coursework. On the way they noticed a poster about the debating club and by the time they'd reached Grace's, she'd convinced Daisy and texted Giorgio to join up too. Later, soon after Daisy had finally dragged Grace away from her sketchpad and they'd actually done some coursework, Grace's phone buzzed.

'It's Lucy. I'll see if she'll FaceTime.'

'Hi.' Lucy's face appeared. Daisy noticed it was blotchy but said nothing.

'Daisy, I know I was a bitch to you before, sorry. I'm really glad you're there too. I opened the journal you gave me. I read this bit:

"I have swept away your offences like a cloud, your

sins like the morning mist. Return to me for I have redeemed you." It reminded me of when I was younger.' Grace and Daisy nodded.

'It says it's from Isaiah 44, Verse 2. I know I didn't say earlier when you were on about God and prayers, Grace, but years ago I was given a little Bible from a beach club. I took it to school once and people called me "Jesus Freak". I soon learnt not to mention anything to do with God. In fact, I guess I went to the other extreme. I wanted to fit in with the "It Gang" so I changed my looks and appearance and what I did. Now though, it feels like I betrayed myself. Do you think God really wants me back, even now?' Lucy asked.

'Sure,' Grace nodded, 'that's totally what God's about. We all mess up and he knows that. It's why he's always there for us, no matter what. Just because not everyone has the courage to own up to others about what they now realise was not the best plan doesn't mean they're any better. In God's eyes, we are all the same. None of us can get it all sorted by ourselves, that's why God sent Jesus – he provided the bridge back for us.'

Lucy smiled. 'I know it doesn't mean that I won't have to deal with all the issues I've landed myself with, but I'm glad to know He's there to help me now.'

'He always is, even when we don't want His help.' Grace smiled wryly. 'God knows I've been there. Anyway, I read on the noticeboard that the Head of Activities is looking for a group to be involved in that discussion/ debating club I mentioned. He's calling it "Launch". Do you want to come along with me to the first meeting? Daisy and Giorgio are going as well. I've asked if they'll play at the new club sometimes if it goes ahead.'

'Okay, I suppose,' Lucy said.

'Great, I'll let Mr Wright know,' Grace replied before signing off.

Chapter 13 – Dizzying Days

Mr Wright, Head of Activities, had been pleased, and Grace and Lucy had spent the next few days emailing each other with poster ideas to help him advertise.

'Tuesday tomorrow. First set of test results back.' Lucy looked nervous as she walked with Grace and Daisy on Monday after college. They both nodded but nothing was said as Lucy's bus arrived. She was going into town to do the food shopping.

On Tuesday morning, Lucy was late into school. Grace and Daisy were concerned but at break they saw her walking in through the gates. Lucy spotted them and gave the thumbs-up sign. They were relieved. Lucy explained she had to go back for two repeat blood tests before Christmas but so far all was clear.

'One of these tests was because I stupidly allowed myself to be persuaded to have a tattoo done by a friend of... that boy...' She could not bring herself to speak his name at that moment. 'I am just glad it was some time ago because you have to wait six months for this test. I don't think I could bear this going on until March.'

'How's your mum doing?' asked Grace.

'Better thanks,' replied Lucy, 'she's found a counsellor who's helping her talk things through. She understands things more now. I don't think her generation were given as much information as we are now. Not that I took much notice. Well, not 'til now.' They moved on to talk about

Launch. The first session was to be on Friday.

During the afternoon at college, Daisy went to meet Giorgio to practise playing for Launch. She'd skipped a class that had been rearranged to do this but when she arrived, he wasn't there. She waited. Honestly, she thought, you'd think he'd be on time. I guess he doesn't know I've skipped class, but well... She checked her phone. No message and only half an hour until her next class. She couldn't miss English so she decided to give him ten more minutes. After that, it wouldn't be worth practising. Argh, he could be so frustrating.

Ten minutes later, her phone buzzed. "Hey, I'm not gonna make the practice. Meet after college and then do you want to come over for a meal at mine around 7 p.m.?" She should say no. She really should. She'd love to see him though and go back with him. She liked his family and loved their food. But then he'd think it was okay to mess her about if she said yes. He hadn't even apologised or explained why. What should she say? She started typing: "Busy tonight..." That was a lie. She deleted it. She wanted to go. But should she? The school clock struck. Time for her next lesson. "Okay," she text and sent it before she could change her mind.

Later she met Giorgio in the music room. She wanted to ask him why he'd cancelled earlier but she was so glad to see him, she didn't want to sound whiney or ruin the afternoon. Why didn't he explain? she thought. He hadn't even mentioned it. She kept quiet and they practised a song they thought they might use at Launch.

Having checked with her parents that it was okay, Daisy joined Giorgio and his family for supper. She hoped she'd have time to ask him about the music session before they ate, but when she arrived, Giorgio's dad greeted her.

'Baked lamb – "kleftiko" my wife calls it! It's cooked all day in the bottom of the range.' Giuseppe proudly carried the ladened dish to the table.

The meat was tender and studded with garlic and sprigs of rosemary; it melted in the mouth and was delicious. Eager to show her thanks, Daisy promised them a pot of japonica jelly she'd made at the weekend. It was a recipe her gran had given her and she hoped Giorgio's family would enjoy it. They were delighted.

For dessert, Giorgio's dad invited them to choose their favourite flavours of ice-cream and brought cornets overflowing with fresh creamy scoops back to the table. To follow, there were tiny cups of strong thick Greek coffee served with honey. Daisy's taste buds were alive with yet another sumptuous feast.

The nights were beginning to close in but they still had time to go to the lake for a short walk. As they neared the shore, Giorgio took Daisy's hand in his. It felt as though electricity had lit her body and she looked down at his hand to see if he'd felt the power of his touch as she had. He gave no sign of it. Was this normal? It wasn't like she'd had much experience apart from a few minor flirtations at school, which amounted to nothing whatsoever. Again, she wondered why he didn't explain his change of plan earlier, but she didn't want to spoil the moment by asking.

The walk was all too short; before long he'd walked her home and they were at her gate again. He leaned towards her and she felt he was about to kiss her, but instead he gave her a brief hug, said ciao and left with a wave. Didn't he want to kiss her? Daisy felt frustration rise within her as she waved back. Why hadn't he kissed her? It had been a lovely evening though, and she supposed it wasn't long until Launch. She probably wouldn't be alone with him but still, it was only a week; maybe then.

Chapter 14 – Days of Delay

'Daisy,' Dad called on Friday morning, 'Mum's eye check is later today. We'll be at the hospital so we'll pick up Rosie after the hospital appointment.'

'Great, thanks.' Excellent! She wouldn't be late for the first session of the new club now.

Launch attracted far more students than they'd expected. Mr Wright and Miss Dale were impressed with the debate topics Grace and Lucy had planned. They handed them round for discussion the following week.

It was also agreed to have music and refreshments in future.

'Hmm.' Daisy raised her eyebrows at them.

'How did Giorgio and I get "volunteered" for the music and refreshments?' she said as she left with Grace and Lucy, who were feigning ignorance. More time with Giorgio though. A warm glow swept through her. It was good news when Daisy arrived home; Mum's eyes were now completely better. 'I'm so glad,' she told Mum, hugging her. 'You've been a great help.'

'Oh Mum, I've only helped a bit. I just can't believe how you usually manage everything. I will try and help more. I never realised there was so much to do.'

Mum smiled. 'I can be ratty sometimes, and so can Dad. There are days when it's all a bit much juggling work, the house, you lot. I expect you'll be the same one day. Now I must get on.' She always did that, just when

Daisy thought she could have a proper conversation with her about things that mattered.

Daisy thought back to when she was little when Mum had shouted rather a lot, mostly before she'd gone back to work. Those had been difficult days; Mum yelling, Dad being silent. Would she be like Mum? Why was it so difficult? She really would like to ask her. Would she be ratty if she worked and ran a home and family? Did she want to do all that? Would she be rattier if she didn't work, like Mum seemed to be? What about Grace's mum? She seemed to love being at home; of course, she worked jolly hard there.

Daisy wandered into the kitchen thinking she might pursue the conversation but Mum had gone upstairs with Rosie. She'd thought about teaching music and would like a family, but could she manage all Mum did? She supposed it depended how things were shared out. She wondered what Grace thought and what it would be like to do that with Giorgio. Hmm... he wasn't always reliable. Eek! She was racing ahead there. He hadn't even kissed her yet. Every week she hoped for the kiss but half-term came and went without it. She supposed she should value the respect but still, she'd love him to kiss her, then she'd know it was more than just friends. Perhaps he did just think of her as a friend? But then he didn't hold hands with Grace. Maybe on Tuesday evening.

The debating club was going so well it had been decided to have a competition, so Tuesdays were now a regular event. Two Tuesday evenings came and went.

Daisy didn't say anything. Giorgio wasn't there the following Tuesday; he'd said he had to work in the café. As they were leaving, Grace caught up with Daisy.

'I can't believe how the weeks have zoomed; it's the debate final soon. Can you run through plans with me? Do you have time to go to the café now?' Daisy nodded, hoping Giorgio would be there.

Daisy scanned the café when they arrived, they found seats but there was no sign of Giorgio. She tried to listen to Grace but her eyes kept wandering to the counter to see if she could glimpse him through the curtain behind. No sign. Why wasn't he there? She thought he said he was working tonight. If he wasn't there, where was he? Was he trying to avoid her?

'Daisy!' She jumped at Grace's voice. 'You seem miles away, what's up?'

'Er, nothing.' Daisy forced herself to concentrate and they soon had the plans for the final sorted. As they were leaving, Daisy caught sight of Giorgio serving behind the counter. Why hadn't he come to talk to her? She sighed.

'Come on, Daisy, what's going on with you?' Grace said, 'You're really not yourself.'

'Oh, I'm just being stupid.' Daisy hid her face in her hands.

'If something's bothering you this much, I doubt it's stupid – try me.' Grace waited.

'It's Giorgio,' Daisy muttered, moving her hands away from her face.

'I thought it might be. What's up, have you guys

rowed?'

'No! That's just it, I kind of wish we had. It's just his communication is either nonexistent or totally confusing, and I never know where I am with him.' Daisy's voice rose with agitation.

'Why? What...' began Grace.

'He said he was working here.' Daisy raised her eyes as she spoke. 'That's why he was missing the debate, then I couldn't see him earlier and when I did, he didn't come out and speak. It just makes me wonder if he's really bothered at all. I mean, I thought he liked me but maybe not. And anyway, where was he if not at the café? What...'

'Daisy, stop. Don't jump to random conclusions. Why don't you ask him?'

'Why doesn't he just tell me? Why should I go back and run after him? Guys always seem to expect that. Why can't he make a bit more effort? No way am I chasing him. It's easy for you, Grace, you're so confident. I'd be way too embarrassed. I know these days it's meant to be cool for girls to do the asking and all that, but chasing guys? It's meant to put them off, isn't it?' Grace was silent as she looked at Daisy.

'Grace?' Daisy was amazed to see tears in her friend's eyes.

Grace stopped and turned, swiping tears away with her sleeve.

'Grace, what's up?' Daisy was alarmed; she'd never seen Grace emotional like this, or at all really. Panic flared up.

'What did I say?' She took a step nearer to Grace.

'It's not easy for me, Daisy, not at all.' Grace hesitated. 'That, well, that someone I said I liked, he doesn't even seem to realise I exist, not as anything more than a childhood friend anyway. He's at uni now but before he went, I visited him and took a kind of "Uni Survival Kit", kind of as a joke, but also hoping he'd think about leaving me behind and maybe see me differently. Well, that didn't happen, and now after what you've said, I think I may have driven him away.' Daisy put her arm around Grace.

'The thing is, I had this boyfriend last year and he said I just didn't seem keen enough, so that didn't last. I mean, after the teacher thing, I told you about how I was trying to be super cool, then apparently I'm too cool! Really? How is anyone supposed to know how to be?' Grace put her head in her hands.

'Grace, I'm so sorry. I didn't mean to upset you. I didn't know. Why didn't you say? Have you been in touch since?'

'Like you say, it's not easy, is it?' Grace gave a watery smile.

Daisy hugged her friend. 'Why don't we do something fun, just the two of us? Tomorrow after college. Take a break from all this boy stuff. I'll ask if I can have the car and we could go late night shopping?'

'Yeah, that'd be great. I haven't been shopping for clothes for ages. Maybe I'll get a new top for the Launch final.'

The girls had great fun shopping. They'd banned

themselves from discussing guys and treated themselves to mocktails to celebrate their new purchases before they left.

Chapter 15 – Day of Decision

Music practices with Giorgio came and went, but as delightful as they were, they'd still never talked about their relationship. Daisy stressed about this; part of her was irritated that he didn't say anything and part was terrified of losing what she had with him now. Overall though, she wanted to risk asking in the hope of finding out how he really felt about her. Perhaps she'd find the right opportunity shortly.

The weeks raced by and soon plans for the end of term debate final competition were in progress. Giorgio and Daisy were providing the entertainment as usual but at the last minute he messaged her. "Hey Daisy, not gonna make it tonight after all but you'll be cool. Hope it goes well. Catch you later." He'd dipped out, again. Why? He hadn't even said why? She would not be "cool". It wouldn't go well, and what did he mean? "Catch you later"? When would his later be? AAARGH! He was sooo annoying! Why was it like she was the only one who communicated? She hated that. It made her look needy. Why couldn't he just explain?

Daisy began to type then stopped. What if this was just an excuse? What if he'd had enough and was trying to let her down gently? No, he wouldn't let the club down. There must a reason. She typed "What's up?" and waited. There was no response. Perhaps he'd put his phone down for a minute, she thought. Daisy waited all day but still received no response. She was not texting again, she decided. She was not going to run after him. An expletive popped into her head. She'd go this evening but she wasn't playing alone. She'd see if they could play their recording. Eugh! She'd have to go and see Mr Wright now and she really didn't have time.

Daisy checked her phone. Only an hour until the debate. Coffee urns to set up, cake to put out, as well as sorting the music out by herself now. Daisy rammed her phone in her bag. Why was he so unreliable? Didn't he care about her? She wished she could talk to Jonno about this stuff, if only he'd message. She guessed he must be tied up with work or out of signal range, knowing he could only use the ship's communication in times of emergency. She ran towards the music department and straight into Mr Wright.

'Whoa, Daisy, what's the hurry?' Daisy's face flushed.

'Well, it looks like it's just me tonight, so I was going to ask if we can play our recording through the phone?'

'You know you could just play on your own, Daisy, you're really good now. I hear from Mrs Stringer that you've started playing some jazz pieces. In her view, you are exceptionally talented.' Daisy blushed but shook her head. Mr Wright persisted.

'Daisy, playing here is a great opportunity for you to build your confidence. I mean, you've played so often in front of the debating club anyway. I'll set out the refreshments, you fetch your harp.'

Daisy felt a surge of fear followed by a wave of

irritation. Why not? It did seem mean to let everyone down. She knew they'd say they preferred the live music. Why should she rely on Giorgio to play music with? It's not like he was reliable anyway! Perhaps he'd think about that if she played without him. In a flash of anger, Daisy nodded and swept off to collect her harp from the music room before she could change her mind. The students began to drift in.

'No Giorgio? Where is he, Daisy?'

'Who knows?' she shrugged, turning away to adjust the keys on her harp.

Mr Wright nodded to indicate he wanted her to begin. Daisy froze. Her fingers wouldn't move. She looked at Mr Wright and he smiled encouragingly. Somehow, she managed to pluck the first string and after that she was lost in the music. Daisy went bright red when the students cheered her. She looked down coyly but inside she felt like she was on a mountain top. When the debate began, Daisy slipped away. She'd done her bit now. She would have liked to hear how Lucy got on but she couldn't face any more questions about Giorgio.

Her route home took her past the café so she looked in to see if Giorgio was there. He was in the window chatting to a guy; not even one of his brothers.

Hah, so he had time to do that but not to keep his commitment to me, she thought. Her fingers slammed into the buttons on her phone. "I see you're really busy this evening!" Send. The second she'd sent it, she regretted it. He'd think she was stalking him now. Why was she such an idiot?

"Hey Daisy, what's that about? I'm helping at the café because my uncle has a problem my dad needs to help him with. It can't wait. My uncle is still here. Are you annoyed with me for helping my family?" Always a reason, always someone else who needs him. So she wasn't allowed to be annoyed if she missed out? How was she supposed to know when he said nothing? Now she felt bad... but why should she? "You could have told me earlier. Would that have been too much for you to do? It isn't the first time. Why do you find it so hard to communicate?" Conflict messaging. Bad news. The thought was ignored as she pressed send and hurried on home. Who did he think he was? Did he think she'd just be there waiting? She checked her phone. Nothing. Had she overreacted? Perhaps it was a real family crisis. Look how kind he'd been when Mum's eyes were bad. She didn't want to lose him. Lose what? What was it they had anyway? Tears pricked at her eyes. She blinked as she went through the front door.

'Hi,' Daisy called, then slunk into her room. Her phone buzzed. "Hey Daisy. I have to go, catch you later." Yeah, in your dreams, she thought. "Jonno," she messaged, "where are you? So annoyed with Giorgio, the guy I mentioned. It feels like he's really messing with my head and my heart. I know I said it wasn't like that but, well, a lot has happened since we last caught up. I need your advice. I hope you're having fun but please message me as soon as possible. Love Daze xx"

After her day, she didn't want to eat dinner or to speak anyone, but she forced herself to sit at the table with her family and eat as much as she could stomach.

'Not hungry?' Mum said. Daisy muttered something about being tired and having an early night.

She went back to her room, grabbed Ted from the wardrobe and hugged him hard against the dull ache in her chest. She flopped on her bed. Why did she feel so terrible? It was like someone had smacked her in the heart. Why did this happen whenever she tried to put forward her point of view? She always ended up feeling bad. She expected Giorgio would yell at her now or just ignore her. She wasn't sure which would be worse. She wondered what would Grace do.

Her eyes went to her childhood Bible laying open on her bedside table and a sentence jumped out at her: "The Lord is close to the broken-hearted." Tears filled Daisy's eyes and careered down her cheeks, dripping onto her quilt. She didn't want to carry on being angry with Giorgio but she did need to know where she stood.

Dad knocked on the door.

'Daisy,' he called. 'Your friend Giorgio, he's downstairs.' Daisy felt hot and cold. He's here? Would he be mad? Should she go down? She rapidly scrubbed her face and headed gingerly down the stairs.

'Hey Daisy, shall we take a walk?'

Daisy nodded, her eyes searching the floor. She hoped he couldn't see she'd been crying.

They were silent as they walked. Why doesn't he

speak? She must say something. She wanted to scream at him though, so she daren't open her mouth. As they were about to cross the bridge near the lake, she stopped. She felt sick and held onto the bridge handrail to steady herself. She shivered and he went to put his arm around her but she shrank back. He looked hurt and began to back away. No!

'Giorgio.' He turned and started walking in the opposite direction. 'Giorgio!' she called. He kept on walking. Well, she wasn't going after him. She called him again and he ignored her. She turned and walked in the opposite direction. It was the wrong way home but she wasn't going to follow him.

'Not much fun being shunned, is it?'

She turned, hardly believing the bitter tone of his voice. It was so unlike him. He was walking towards her now and he looked pretty mad. She flashed back to the way she'd seen him look at his brother at the café that day. Did she really know him at all? Maybe he wasn't the guy she thought he was. Daisy felt like crying. She tried to stop the tears but they fell anyway. He spoke gently now.

'I am trying, Daisy, I really am, but you need to understand boys can feel unsure too. I had a pretty rough time with my last girlfriend and I don't want anything like that to happen again.'

'I don't know what happened but whatever it was, it's no good if it gets in the way of us. I mean, is there an us? I need to know.' What are you saying? a voice screamed in her head. Shut up, shut up. She didn't shut up though.

'Are we just friends or what? I need to know. I can't deal with not knowing.' There, she'd said it. Now he'd probably rant at her, say she was too needy or defensive, that she gets upset over nothing, or he'd ignore her until she felt guilted into saying she was wrong. Perhaps she should... SHUT UP. Daisy tried to turn off the internal dialogue. She went quiet and looked at the ground. Swallow me now, she pleaded. She steeled herself. Would he be angry or walk away?

Giorgio gently pulled her towards him. This time she stayed close, but her heart was beating as if a million butterflies were trying to escape.

'Hey Daisy, I really care about you, but our family, it's complicated. My uncle's family has a challenging situation and, well, I'm needed to help at the café sometimes if my brother has to assist Uncle Giacomo.'

'What kind of challenges? I mean, I don't want to pry but I'm trying to understand.'

'Uncle G has some mental health issues and there are times he needs support. We don't always have any notice of this.'

Daisy realised there was so much she still didn't know about him, so she continued, 'Does he have help from anywhere else? I mean, like, medically?'

'Yes, but he's having a hard time accepting that. I think it's a generation thing. Anyway, sometimes he thinks he can cope and then, well, we find he's not managing, and so...'

'I kind of understand. It's a bit like when Mum had

her accident and I was needed to help at home more. You and Grace were so understanding then. I'm sorry. I shouldn't have jumped to conclusions. It would have helped to know before though.'

'Hey, no, I guess I can understand why and I'm sorry. You're right, I should communicate more but like I said, it's not always easy. I know I can't expect you to mindread. I'll work on it, Daisy, but you need to ask me if you need to know.'

Daisy knew in her heart she did need to speak out more. She was afraid too but she'd warmed with his reassurance. Could she trust him? She looked up. His eyes held her gaze. She thought she could trust him.

'That would be great.' She gave him a watery smile, tilting her chin up, then felt his lips on hers. The kiss was worth waiting for. It was, she thought, even better than she'd imagined. And she had a great imagination.

Chapter 16 – Delectable Days

'Listen up,' Mr Wright began at the now thriving debating club. 'The knockout system is over and I have the results of the finalists. First though, I want to say Miss Dale and I were really impressed with the quality of the debates and the research which you all clearly put in. The content has been excellent.' Everyone grinned back. 'Now, the final two competitors are: Lucy Turner and Barnabus – Barny – Abrahams. The topic will be pinned to the board shortly and we're rewarding you with a bit of a party afterwards. Daisy and Giorgio, you can have a night off from refreshments, but we'd appreciate your music please.' There were cheers and whoops. Lucy went red. Barny just nodded.

'The topic is "Creation Not Evolution" – Lucy will be for this topic, Barny against,' Miss Dale said.

'He has razor-sharp debating techniques, I heard him in the semi-final. I feel so intimidated,' Lucy whispered to Grace and Daisy.

'You're on solid ground and sound in your argument. There's no reason why you can't win the day,' Grace assured her.

'Really?' Lucy wasn't convinced.

'Really. Pray for confidence, although I guess this won't be at the top of the list.' Grace had gone with Lucy last Tuesday for the second lot of tests.

'Yep. The results come out next Tuesday, one day

before the debate final.' Grace watched her put her hands together like at school prayer time. Lucy gave a half smile and Daisy mouthed, "All the best". Daisy and Giorgio were going to the debate, both looking forward to it and to providing the music afterwards. Daisy was also feeling sad though. It was nearly the end of term. She would really miss Giorgio during the holidays. There were no plans yet to meet up and she found herself again wondering if she'd read more into their relationship than was really there. She'd sent another message to Jonno telling him that the "crisis" was over but she still longed to catch up with him. Chats with him helped her emotional perspective.

Grace was haring around, frenzied during the penultimate week of term. She kept calling Daisy to help her organise various things for the debate final; find extra chairs, contact the lighting and sound technicians, and tons of stuff that Daisy hadn't even realised would be needed. She wasn't surprised when her mobile showed Grace ringing for the third time that Thursday evening but she was beginning to feel a little worn down by it all. She didn't like to admit it but she was a bit irritated as it kept interrupting her music practice.

'Yes,' she answered less than enthusiastically.

'I need you to help me out of a tight spot, please.' Not another one, thought Daisy, recalling how Grace had spent half the morning sketching.

'It's my aunt,' continued Grace, 'Aunt Alice, she's given to bonkers ideas and has just phoned my mother.

She said she's taking off on a cruise to Alaska for a week in the Christmas hols and needs her log cabin minded. Mum volunteered me but it's a grim place to be alone. Can you come? I wondered about asking Giorgio too.'

Daisy could barely contain her excitement. She was glad now that Giorgio was not overtly her boyfriend – her parents would in no way agree to such a plan if that was the case, but as they saw him as a friend of Grace's perhaps it would be okay?

'I'd love to,' enthused Daisy, 'I'll need to check with my parents though. Can I let you know tomorrow? Will you ask Giorgio?'

'Yes,' Grace replied. 'That's fine. We break up on the 15th and we'd need to leave for the cabin on the 16th, back on the 23rd. Her cabin has electricity, hot and cold running water and a functioning bathroom, but otherwise it's pretty basic. We'll need to take sleeping bags. My aunt has left funds for supplies as her thanks for looking after the cabin. Oh and it's on the edge of the Cheviots in a woody bit but you can sometimes get mobile signals.'

Daisy prayed her parents would agree.

In the end, they needed some persuasion, but they'd grown to trust Grace with her open countenance and straightforward ways. They also liked Giorgio and were delighted Daisy spent so much time practising the harp with him so, finally, they agreed. Yes! Daisy silently cheered. Immediately she set about making a packing list.

Grace caught up with Daisy late on Friday afternoon just as she was leaving college. 'Can you come to the café with me? Giorgio said he'd let us know if he can go later. He said to call in for coffee.'

'Sure.' Daisy hadn't seen Giorgio much since Tuesday so she was pleased.

It was dark as they walked down towards the café and they were glad to see the glow of the lights inviting them into its warmth. Fresh coffee scented the air and as they made their way to the counter, Giorgio's mum drew a tray of almond pastries out of the oven.

Sitting in the squishy russet-coloured leather chairs, they munched the delicious baking and sipped hot lattes.

Daisy loved the atmosphere in the café; it was so relaxing and it had been ages since she and Grace had had time to chill out together. This was lovely. They hardly noticed the time go by until Giorgio appeared. It was nearly 5.30 p.m.

'It's fine for the cabin,' said Giorgio, 'I just had to negotiate with Yannis to cover my shifts as we usually both work here in the holidays. He needs the money for his boating scheme though so he didn't strike too hard a deal!'

Yes! Yes! Yes! Daisy only just managed not to shout out loud with glee.

'How do we get there?' she asked.

'Train,' said Grace, 'then a taxi. It's a fairly straightforward journey, I've done it often with my brothers. My aunt is footing the fares too – she insists. All part of the appreciation.'

They discussed what they'd need for a while then

Grace said she had to head off to finish the details for the debate final. Daisy would have liked to have stayed but knew she needed to be home as her parents wanted her to babysit her sister that night. It would be the first night out they'd had together since Mum had recovered. She wasn't about to anger them and put this cabin week in jeopardy.

Daisy awoke late to a surprise on Saturday morning. Her mum called up the stairs to say Giorgio was at the door. Nothing had been planned for the weekend and Daisy had expected to be working on her English assignment; it was due on Monday, but that could wait. She'd nearly finished it anyway. Quickly throwing on her robe (a new satin one she'd bought when she and Grace went shopping), she forced herself to walk downstairs rather than rushing as her heart bid her.

'Hi,' she called in what she hoped was a casual manner.

'Hi,' echoed Giorgio,

'I have an unexpected day free from the café. The sun's shining so I wondered if you would like to join me at the lake? We could take the boat out to the island.' Daisy glanced at her mum, who was watering plants in the hallway.

'That's fine by me as long as you are home for tea tonight, please. Gran is coming.'

'Thanks, Mum.'

'Just the two of you?' Mum looked up, her eyebrows raised.

'Oh it's not like that Mum!' Daisy shot back, anxious

not to ruin the cabin trip.

'I'll just be a few minutes,' Daisy called to Giorgio while taking the stairs two at a time, 'go into the sitting room and make yourself at home.'

When Daisy was ready, she and Giorgio made their way to the lake. He stopped off at the café and went in for a few moments, returning with a huge picnic basket. Daisy smiled. She knew he was fond of his food but this was thoughtful too.

Having loaded the basket and themselves into the boat, Giorgio rowed across to the island. They pulled the boat high up onto the beach as the weather could be unpredictable, especially in December. Taking bottles of juice, they left the basket at the base of a large pine tree. There was a longer beach on the far side of the island so they took a lengthy hike through a wood and flopped onto the sandy beach. There was a light breeze so they backed up to a little cove overhung with pines forming a natural tent.

Stroking the sandy floor, Daisy looked out towards the tiny dunes peppered with tussocks of pampas grass to the left. As the wind picked up, the dunes rippled and seemed to take flight, rising into peaks; rivulets of sand slid down, slithering along like snake trails. In the distance, soft crescents had formed. Daisy pointed them out to Giorgio. He told her about Uncle Antonio, a great traveller and anthropologist who'd spent time with the Bedouin researching ancient routes.

'Uncle Antonio used to say, I think, that crescents

indicated a time of change. I hope this doesn't mean we are in for a storm.' They thought they might need to be near the boat in case the weather changed, so they headed back to the other shore.

Thankfully, the wind had dropped and they were able to enjoy their picnic bathed in winter sunlight. They chatted as they ate their Mediterranean-style food.

'Delicious,' said Daisy. 'Literally no stale sausage rolls and curled up sandwiches here.' Giorgio grinned.

The early sunset showered the landscape in a warm orange light and Daisy knew they would soon need to go back. Just as she was about to jump to her feet, Giorgio took her hand.

'I really like you, Daisy,' he began, 'but I don't know how you feel about me?'

Daisy looked at him astounded. It must be obvious that she was smitten? 'I mean, what you said to your mum about...'

She reached his hand and squeezed it gently.

'I really like you too, Giorgio,' she said shyly, 'I just didn't want my mum to worry about the cabin trip.'

Giorgio relaxed. He put his arm around her and drew her close. Daisy longed for him to kiss her again and leaned towards him, but he hesitated.

'I think it's important we move slowly. I know how I am and I don't want to spoil things for us or cause any concern for your parents by rushing ahead.'

Daisy wasn't sure quite what he meant. She felt somehow disappointed. All too soon, he pulled her to her feet.

'We must go before the light fades.'

Daisy looked at the sky. It seemed exceptionally dark now, though not yet dusk. As they neared the boat, tiny hail stones began pelting them.

'Really? Hail? Who knew?' Giorgio grabbed a small tarpaulin from the back of the boat, which he unrolled so he and Daisy had a bit of shelter as they headed back.

It was like a legion of tin soldiers drumming as they crouched under their makeshift roof while trying to row across the now choppy lake. It was taking much longer than the trip out. Daisy began to worry about the time. She didn't want her parents to ban her from the cabin trip.

'How far now?' she asked.

'Hard to say.' Giorgio stuck his head out from under the tarpaulin. 'It's hailing so much I can't see. Don't worry, we'll be okay.'

She wanted to seem cool, not someone who had to get in by curfew, so she just said, 'Okay.' She tried to estimate the time in her head as she'd left her phone back at the café, not wanting to lose it in the water. That meant she'd have to take time going back to fetch it too. If she was late, her parents would stop her going on the trip. Her mind began to race in circles of increasing fear of losing out.

Daisy put her hand to her mouth as her stomach began to churn and nausea rose. She dropped her head, hoping Giorgio wouldn't notice as she began the breathing exercises that she'd learnt with Jonno. She didn't want to have a panic attack. Inhale, exhale, in... She took a sudden breath in as the boat bumped.

'That's us back, thankfully,' said Giorgio as they arrived at the shore.

It was just going dark as they hurried to the café. Daisy grabbed her phone and checked the time. She relaxed as she saw there was still half an hour before she needed to be home. They enjoyed a hot chocolate together then Giorgio offered to walk her back. As they left the café, lights twinkled under the octopus-ink sky as if mirroring the star-studded black velvet canopy that sheltered them while they walked. Daisy could not have imagined a more perfect day. Well, perhaps if there had been another kiss, but hopefully there would be soon. Not long to go before they'd be at the cabin.

Giorgio hugged her at the gate. Perhaps it was her imagination but he seemed reluctant to let her go. He moved away after a long hug. Then with his customary ciao and a wave, he was off back to the café.

Later that evening as Daisy snuggled under her duvet, her phone beeped. She grinned when she saw it was Jonno. "Hi," she messaged back, "can you FaceTime?" Her phone buzzed and Jonno's blue eyes shone out. They spent a happy hour catching up. He'd been up in the Arctic Circle on the ship with no mobile signal. Daisy had known there'd be a reason for his silence. He was back at port now for a day before heading off again. She wondered how he managed to adapt to all the different time zones and cultures. She found it hard enough when the clocks changed here. Daisy told Jonno about the cabin and he teased her about her budding romance, but she felt pleased. It meant he thought there was at least something a bit special about her relationship with Giorgio.

'Tell me a bit more about this Giorgio, what's he like exactly? And Grace, I want to hear about your BF at Waterside.'

'Grace is amazing, you'd like her. Of course, she'll never take your place as BFF boy, no-one could, but she's fun to be with like you. Optimistic like you. She's great at solving problems as long as they're not to do with her studies. She hates to study – not like you, superbrain. She loves art though and spends literally half her life with her head in her sketchbook. She's a good friend too and she was really kind to me in the early days when the mean girl squad were at large. She's tall, probably as tall as you, and has hazel eyes that kind of smile at you and long wavy hair the same colour as yours. She seems super confident but says she's not underneath. She's great at saying what she feels, in a good way.'

'I like the sound of her. Pity she's not a guy. So, what about the latest love of your life?'

'Giorgio? He's gorgeous, of course.'

'Of course.'

'Wavy black hair, melting milk chocolate eyes.'

'Enough already – get me his number, lol!'

'Haha – he's mine! Or I'd like him to be. He's taller than me, quite athletic and has olive skin. No beard and well, yeah, like I say, gorgeous.'

'Okay, but what's he like as a person? Give me the lowdown.'

'So, totally different from you there. You are literally the best boy communicator I know, whereas getting info out of him is like, well, to be honest, he's not exactly emo to say the least. He's okay though, when you can get him to talk, he's quite passionate...'

A snorty giggle from Jonno stopped her in her tracks.

'No, not like that – well, not yet.' She giggled. 'I mean, when you get him to talk he does tell you what he feels. He's really chillaxed too, you'd like that about him, although it does mean arrangements can be, shall we say, rather fluid.'

'Ah Daze, you always did like a plan. Take care though,' he said. 'Don't let yourself get too deep in too soon. I don't want to see you hurt. Also, remember your music. Don't let your dreams go.'

Jonno was the only one other than Mrs Stringer she'd told about her dream to play the jazz harp after the putdown at Meadow Lane.

'A while ago, I saw a set of scores for the jazz harp in one of the music rooms so I asked my music tutor Mrs Stringer about them.'

'Go on.'

'She told me there is a jazz trio group and suggested I join. The plan is to go for an introduction tomorrow.'

Well, that was her plan now. She'd literally just made a mental note to message Mrs Stringer after the FaceTime. She hadn't wanted to commit herself when she'd first been asked as she had hoped she might be invited for lunch at Giorgio's after church. Jonno's comments had made her rethink though. She should go and join the trio and not always be available in case Giorgio was free.

'Good for you, Daze. Your dreams are important. Keep hold of them, girl.'

'Sure thing. Also, I plucked up the courage to play solo at the debating club. So no,' she said, with honesty now, 'I'm not forgetting my music. Hey, how about Carlos?'

'Sad times, we're on different boats for the next trip. We are hoping to rent a flat for shore leave though so that's to look forward to after his next cruise.'

'Well, bon voyage and all the best with the flat,' Daisy replied.

'Okay then. Chillax, girlfriend,' he said. His signature sign-off reminded her not to worry too much; he knew what she was like. They promised to message again soon so he could hear about her trip.

When Daisy lay back down she relived the day before falling into a sweet sleep dreaming of picnics, boats and crescents.

Chapter 17 – December Days

On Sunday morning, Lucy stood outside Willows Church. She looks as nervous as I did when I first came to this church, Daisy thought. She joined her to wait for Grace, who despite still working frantically with the debate final arrangements had texted Lucy to see how she was doing. She'd remembered about Lucy's final test results being due the coming week and had invited her to church.

'I'm scared of church,' she told Daisy, 'I get that God still loves me but I'm scared of the people in churches. They can be so, well, self-righteous in my experience. I'm more scared about the test results though and you guys have been so helpful, so here I am.'

At one minute to ten, Grace flew up the path. 'I did leave early but the geese got out again,' she protested breathlessly.

As they went in, soft music was playing and a few people in black clothes walked onto the stage. Sitting near the back on comfortable chairs, they watched a mime drama evolve. One person was acting God and others brought lavish gifts, which they placed at His feet. The final person appeared with nothing, but cleverly mimed folding himself and offering himself to God. God was delighted and welcomed him with open arms. Then an instrumental track was played by the band on stage. Daisy noticed Lucy had tears coursing down her face but kindly looked away as Lucy rubbed her cheeks with her sleeve.

The verse from the Bible was the one from Isaiah that Grace had written in Lucy's journal about returning to God. Daisy felt goosebumps prickle all over her as she listened. A few lively praise choruses were sung, then the pastor prayed and said a blessing.

The service had been quite short and Daisy had really enjoyed it. It was nothing like the formal experiences she had endured before. Afterwards, they headed off for coffee and a look at the bookshop. Grace gently asked Lucy how she was feeling.

'I'm still pretty terrified about Tuesday but everyone's been really kind.' She seemed surprised.

'If you wouldn't feel too uncomfortable, I wondered if you would like to ask the pastor to pray for you? You needn't say why, he won't ask, just that you would like prayer for next Tuesday.'

'I guess, but I feel really embarrassed to ask.'

'Well, how about we write a request in the prayer book? You don't need to give details or even put your name.' Grace's gentle suggestion had touched her heart and Lucy crumpled into sobs. She nodded. Daisy could see her hands shaking as she wrote.

'I still feel scared but somehow a little stronger inside,' she said as she put the pen down.

Daisy felt pretty nervous herself as she made her way to Mrs Stringer's house where the trio practised. She felt like backing off but forced herself to knock on the door. Mrs Stringer welcomed her in and introduced her to Phil, who played the saxophone. Mrs Stringer on the trumpet made up the trio, with a harp for Daisy to use. As they started with a familiar piece, Daisy found she was really enjoying this. The others were keen for her to join them as they'd recently lost their old harpist. It would mean regular practice on Sunday afternoons as they had several gigs in December, which would cut out any lunches with Giorgio.

Will he still like me if I don't go to lunch? A small voice piped up in her head. Don't be ridiculous, she replied to herself, are you going to spend your life only doing what you think others want you to do? What about your dreams and ideas? Yes, but I want Giorgio, he's part of my dreams... Yes, the dialogue continued, but if he's really the man for you, don't you think he'd want you to fulfil your dreams? You don't want to spend your life regretting turning down this opportunity; it's not as if your parents are likely to present you with another one. Daisy took a deep breath and decided she'd join the trio.

Chapter 18 – Debating Days

Daisy knew Monday would be a really hard day for Lucy. At lunchtime, she saw her walking up and down the field outside the gates and joined her.

'How are you doing?'

'I can't settle. I barely slept and I have to wait until ten o'clock tomorrow morning to call. I don't think I will be able to come into college before though.'

'How about we go to the café first thing? I'll meet you there.'

Lucy nodded. 'Thanks, that would help.'

Next morning, Daisy walked down to the café and ordered a double espresso. She felt she would need her wits about her to help Lucy while she waited to make this call. Giorgio was at college and his mum served her. When Lucy came in, Giorgio's mum came back across. Somehow she seemed to know the girl was troubled and briefly touched her arm as she added two free cantucci biscuits to the saucer with her hot chocolate order. Lucy smiled her thanks.

At five to ten, Lucy walked outside the café and sat on the circular seat that enclosed the plane tree. She dialled the number she now knew by heart. Daisy waited inside the café, silently saying a prayer for Lucy. Moments later, she signalled to Daisy to come out. Daisy left the drinks money on the table and left. I hope everything's okay, she thought. How would she cope with Lucy if it wasn't?

Perhaps she could call Grace to join them? No, she was at the dentist first thing. Oh well, here goes...

'I'm still waiting,' Lucy said, 'I just need someone with me. My legs feel like lead and I think I'm gonna puke. I want to run away but there's nowhere to run. I can hardly run away from myself, can I?' Daisy could see that her eyes looked wild with fear. What should she say? Finally, Lucy turned to the voice on the other end.

'Clear?' Daisy heard her ask.

'Clear for both these last tests?' A moment of silence.

'Thank you, thank you... thanks,' she said again before hanging up.

'Thanks Daisy, and thank you God.' She breathed deeply.

'I must text Grace,' she said, typing into her phone, tears of gratitude plopping onto the screen.

They walked along the shore by the lake as she texted. Lucy bent down to the water and bathed her hot cheeks, rinsing the salty droplets away and cooling her face. Grace came running up, beaming at the news and raised her hands in a silent thanks to God. She hugged Lucy then in true Grace mode began looking ahead.

'All ready for the last study stint for the debate then?'

Lucy gave her a watery smile and nodded.

'So glad to be thinking of the competition again instead of the horrors that have dogged my thoughts lately.'

Daisy had done a splendid job assisting Grace with the organisation and the debating room was all set for Friday.

On Friday morning, Daisy had texted Giorgio to be

sure he would be there. She wasn't so nervous now she practised with the jazz group. In fact, they'd even asked her to do a few more gigs with them in the new year, but it was still important that Giorgio let her know. To her relief, he'd confirmed he would be there. Good progress. She smiled, pleased their communication seemed to be improving.

Giorgio was already waiting in the room when Daisy arrived and had set up their entertainment area.

'I'm going to need to leave early...' Giorgio began. Daisy raised her eyebrows.

'What?'

He crossed his arms. 'I'm going to rugby practice with the boys from church. They play every Wednesday and they asked me to join in tonight as they are short.'

Daisy rubbed the back of her neck. He was so frustrating. What was it with him and keeping a commitment?

'What about the music?' she asked.

'Oh, I will do that, it's just I won't hang around after.'

Daisy dipped her head then quickly raised it. She didn't want him to see her disappointment.

It wasn't like she could expect him to answer to her for every aspect of his social life. It's just that she wished he'd let her know before the last minute when his plans changed. She nodded even though she wanted to throw the music scores at him instead of passing them across. He seemed to have no appreciation of why it might have been nice not to have just landed her with this change of arrangements. Inconsiderate. Thoughtless. Selfish. A rant began in her head. She tried to remember what he'd said during "the bridge row" as she now thought of it. Okay, so he was trying, but in her book he needed to try harder.

Miss Dale was putting out the last of the refreshments so Daisy distracted herself and went to help. Mr Wright had provided a flask of mulled wine and some mince pies. When everyone was there, Miss Dale introduced the debating topic and competitors. Barny kicked off with a convincing argument for why it was ludicrous to still believe in creation and spouted forth with reams of evidence for evolution. Lucy came back strongly with examples of the why creation was still a valid claim. The audience threw questions and the debate went on until it was time for Lucy's concluding point.

'2 Peter 3:8 says: "With the Lord, a day is like a thousand years and a thousand years is like a day." So, I say the creator created but perhaps his six days were as six thousand years or more, which left time for changes that he planned to take place after he initially sparked the creation.'

The vote went narrowly in Lucy's favour, her final point swaying the audience. Grace cheered and the audience clapped and whistled. Daisy clapped but she still felt raw inside. Even her music lacked the usual liveliness. Giorgio left after their short ensemble. The event, however, was a roaring success with further debate carrying on during and after the delicious refreshments until the caretaker called a halt as he needed to lock up.

As Daisy was leaving with Lucy and Grace, Barny caught them up.

'Hey, you're a worthy competitor,' he said to Lucy. 'Can I take you for coffee tomorrow and we can talk about topics for next term?' Lucy looked at Daisy and Grace. They smiled.

'Sure,' she agreed. They planned to meet at the café at 5 p.m. the following day. He sped off.

'Do you think it was a good idea to agree?' she asked. Daisy thought she might be worried what they might think of her.

'Yes!' they said in unison.

'Barny's cool,' Grace said. 'He has a strong faith too. He's in my art and design group. We were chatting the other day and he was telling me about the church he attended in Zambia before he and his dad left to join his step-mum here. He has a passion for his heritage.'

'How can he argue so convincingly against what he believes in?' Lucy asked.

'Well...' Barny appeared from behind her, 'I enjoy looking at opposite points of view. I think it kind of reinforces my beliefs to see what I'm up against.'

'Great for a career in law or politics,' Lucy joked.

'Actually, it develops persuasive skills. I love designing. I want to champion Zambian heritage through textiles. There are so few African designers.'

'Your work is amazing,' Grace said. 'Maybe he can show you sometime, Lucy?'

Grace gave Daisy a knowing look.

'Sure,' said Barny.

Lucy blushed.

Daisy wondered if Lucy was developing a growing interest in Barny, and not just for his debating skills.

Chapter 19 – Days of Dissatisfaction

As Daisy was about to put her light out, a message came through from Giorgio. "Had a great time with the lads, going to make this a regular on Wednesdays." Daisy knew a real relationship was one where two people had separate lives and shared them the same way they did with their family and best friends. So why did she feel so mad that Giorgio made decisions without talking them through when surely he could see they would impact on her? Was she expecting too much too soon? She knew he'd said she should ask him, but sometimes she'd just like him to understand that she needed him to communicate what was happening. Perhaps she should message Jonno first. He always helped her work out what she needed to say. It would be so easy if she could fall in love with Jonno – if he wasn't gay, that was – but they just didn't feel like that about each other; besties, yes, but nothing romantic. Why were relationships so complicated? Perhaps she'd be better off not being involved. She wasn't sure how much of this rollercoaster ride she could take. No! She didn't mean that!

Her phone buzzed. It was Jonno. He must have read her mind. They FaceTimed and Jonno was full of his latest trip and the love of his life. Daisy listened, laughing at his crazy tales and minor scrapes.

'Jonno,' she then began, 'I need to ask you about some boy stuff.'

'Me, dear? Boy stuff, dear?' He joked, then realising she wanted to be serious, he listened. After she'd explained, Jonno was silent for a moment.

'I expect you want me to tell you what to say or do, but you know already. Think about what you said to me about what's important to you.'

'I...' Daisy hesitated, 'I guess I do.' The ship's tannoy boomed out and she knew Jonno had to go. He mimed a kiss and their FaceTime ended.

Chapter 20 – Days to Dream

When Daisy arrived at college on Monday, there was a crowd clustered around the noticeboard. 'Have you seen the notice?' Grace appeared by her side. 'It's an opportunity to take a term abroad in New Zealand! I am so going to apply.' Daisy struggled to the front. She read that there were places available for various subjects and those studying these had been offered a chance to apply. Music, art and business were among the subjects. Her heart hammered. She'd longed for a chance to visit a school in a different country but was really bad at languages, so she'd never thought how this might happen as the cost of flights to Australasia or America were so high. Now she may be able to go to New Zealand on this exchange for a fraction of the cost! Wow!

'Hey, are you free? Let's look at the form together,' Grace suggested.

They headed off to the school snack bar, flipped open their laptops and located the application form on the school site. It explained that a local undergraduate had linked with a primary school in Christchurch and would be going on a placement to help with outdoor activities for a term. The school had quickly offered to extend opportunities to other students from his town on an exchange basis. The undergraduate had suggested Waterside as it was his closest college.

'Let's apply now.' Grace began typing. Grace and

Daisy looked at each other. Daisy hesitated. She wanted to go but was worried about what her parents might say. Also, would Giorgio want to go? Was that really that important? What if she and Grace didn't both get places? Was it really worth her applying?

'Come on, Daisy. Type. It's first come, first served. You don't want to miss out.' She could apply, she supposed. Why should she factor Giorgio in? It wasn't like he would message her to talk about it. And after all, she could back out if she got a place and changed her mind. There were bound to be tons of people wanting to go. She clicked on the form and worked through completing and submitting.

'I hope if I'm offered a place my parents will be okay about it,' she said.

'Me too, although my parents are usually cool about travel opportunities. Two of my brothers took mini gap years to do charity work abroad.'

Daisy decided she'd mention it in passing to her parents later and gauge their reaction, then cross the "battle bridge" if she needed to. Her phone buzzed and she saw Grace had received a message too. It was from Giorgio saying he was applying and wanting to know if they would be as well. Despite her protestations to herself earlier, Daisy suddenly found herself very keen to go. Their laptops dinged and a message came through confirming receipt of their applications and saying that places would be allocated in the Christmas break.

'How frustrating having to wait 'til then,' Grace grimaced.

On Monday, everyone seemed to be talking about the exchange – everyone except Lucy. All she wanted to talk about was Barny. Neither of them had applied to go but apparently over their coffee on Friday they'd hatched plans for entering a county debate. Daisy and Grace tried hard to be interested but they both wanted to talk about their hopes for New Zealand.

'What did your parents say?' Grace asked when Lucy left them to meet Barny.

'They seemed okay. I was surprised but they said it could be a marvellous chance to develop my harp music and have a taste at teaching, which they know is what I'd like to do. I'm not sure if they really believe I'll actually get a place though.'

'Are you interested in teaching music then? I'd really like to teach art. UCAS form final choices have to be in next term. Where are you applying to? Maybe we can both take a teaching degree at the same university?'

'That would be amazing! I'm hoping to get a place at York St John, that's my first choice. They have a great music department, but I'm applying to Hull and Lincoln too. How about you?'

'York St John too and Sheffield, but I doubt I'll get the grades for that. You know what I'm like with my work. Apart from art, of course, and even then the coursework...'

Daisy grinned at her friend. She knew exactly what Grace was like. Always happiest with her head in a sketchbook.

'I do hope we both get places at YSJ then. I'd love that. Maybe we could house share?'

'Oh, that'd be great, but talking of coursework, I've just remembered some history that's due in for tomorrow.' Grace ran off with a hurried wave.

Daisy wondered what Giorgio planned to do. He didn't talk about the future much, she thought, wandering to her next class. She'd like to ask him but didn't want him to think she was trying to pin him down or anything. Daisy recalled her conversation with Jonno about boys and relationships. He'd said they're scared of what a possible relationship might change and think they couldn't be happier than they are right now. It wasn't his view, he'd told her – 'I think if you're interested in someone, why miss out on seeing if things can work out for you to be together? Start to share your hopes and dreams, good times and bad. It's like anything you want to do, you need to show some commitment.' Hmm. She agreed with Jonno but he'd also recommended patience. It looked like she couldn't expect that much with Giorgio, at least not yet. Hopefully, they'd all have time together in New Zealand soon and maybe there'd be a chance on the long flight over. He wouldn't be able to just leave the flight. All she needed now was to get a place. Loads of people had applied. She wondered how many places there were. She wished they could know sooner but at least there was the cabin trip to look forward too. Not long now. She messaged Jonno. "How's the trip so far? Amazing possibility at college to go to NZ next year. Hope I get a place, Giorgio and Grace too. Any chance you'll be going there early in the New Year anytime? It would be amazing to meet up. Love Daze xx"

Chapter 21 – Days of Darkest Winter

Friday soon arrived. Daisy was really excited about setting off for the cabin and rushed home to complete her packing. They set off the following day. It was a long train journey but the three friends hardly noticed the time pass as they caught up on the term's events and talked about Christmas.

'We might be having a party,' Grace said, 'I'm hoping to persuade Mum on this, but my brothers are keen so I expect it'll work out.'

They stopped at the station café where they ate eggs on toast and drank tea while waiting for the taxi to take them to the cabin.

'That's us here,' Grace said as they pulled up by a wooden log building at the edge of a forest. Daisy thought it looked a bit spooky and was glad she was with the others. She wrapped her arms around herself.

It was cold and dark when they arrived but Grace's aunt had left kindling, a box of firelighters and some wood. Grace quickly made up the fire in the rustic log burner while the others explored the cabin. Giorgio was to sleep in the small single room and the girls were to share the larger twin room. Extra blankets sat on wooden trunks at the end of all the beds.

'For warmth, there's no central heating!' Grace explained, catching them up and pointing at the blankets. They headed to the kitchen. Rummaging about in the cupboards, Grace discovered a packet of spaghetti and some tomato sauce.

'It won't be like your mum's, Giorgio,' she chuckled, 'but it's food.'

'Hey,' Giorgio moved towards the cooker, 'let me do that.'

Grace dug out a game of Scrabble and Daisy helped her set it out. They ate what turned out to be a tasty supper and managed half a game before Grace yawned, followed by Daisy.

'I'll wash up, you guys turn in. It's been a long day,' Giorgio volunteered.

The next day, Daisy felt warm as she awoke. The fire was still glowing, woodsmoke scenting the air. Drawing the heavy drapes, she took in the garden blanketed with soft thick snow. Shrubs and tree branches were garlanded with feathery wraps, laying in heaps along the top of the picket fence and decoratively icing the top of the gateposts. It was so quiet, as if the snow had eased nature into winter's slumbering peace. Then the reverie was disturbed as the door burst open and in rushed Grace, flushed pink with the cold, shaking her damp snowy coat. She was followed closely by a laughing Giorgio, who missed her with a large snowball.

'Grace met her target,' Giorgio laughed, brushing snow from his hair.

Daisy had slept until nearly nine and the others had been down the lane to buy breakfast. Sunny rays splashed across the garden path and beyond close-grown trees like freshly hewn pencils staked out the acres, casting a muddy haze over the snow. Occasional evergreens punctuated the leafless expanse beneath. Daisy was enchanted. It didn't seem scary today; more like a winter wonderland. Daisy spied creamy yellow butter and a loaf. She opened the packages and felt it was still warm.

'Yum. Where did you buy this?' she asked.

'My aunt had left a note saying supplies were available at the farm through the wood so we went there first thing, sleepyhead!'

They ate breakfast then Daisy went out to explore. Under a large tree she discovered a swing made from wood. Swishing the snow from the seat, she began swinging gently, a snowy carpet beneath her, the sun briefly glimmering on her face. Daisy felt a warm sense of contentment sweep through her.

They'd been invited for lunch at the farm so they walked back through the swathe of forest that cloaked the southern flank of the nearby hill. Looping around to the stile that straddled the wall, they took the rough track scrambling up snow-dusted, crumbly, rocky patches, then shuffled on their waterproof-clad bottoms to descend the short distance to the farm.

After a splendid lunch, they made their way back with more packages of food. Rough gusts troubled the air, and by the time they reached the cabin, fresh snow was falling. It fell steadily for most of the afternoon so they hunkered down and played some of the many boardgames Grace had rooted out of the old trunk in the sitting room.

Monopoly was the favourite, with competitive bantering as if they were kids.

An early sunset saw the snow cease and shafts of light streamed through the trees, bathing the distant hills in ever deepening shades of apricot. Giorgio and Daisy decided to go for an evening walk while Grace cooked supper. After a while, they made their way back through the trees, kicking up tracks of snow as they went. The light began to fade and they were glad of the trail of smoke billowing from the chimney; a reassurance they were on the right track towards the shelter of the cabin. Giorgio pointed out the various tracks of different animals – squirrel, possibly fox – and then they came across a much larger print. Giorgio looked up confused. He thought it looked like cattle, but surely not? Then as if in confirmation, the low rumble of a long moo sounded not far in front of them. Daisy nearly jumped out of her skin.

Through the trees they could just discern a large white cow, quickly followed by a herd of Cheviot cattle; they'd broken through part of the fence. Behind them they glimpsed more smoke and soon tracked their way to a rickety house. They knocked on the door and were surprised to hear a man call, 'Come in!' Cautiously, Giorgio opened the door and a surprising sight greeted them. The man, about sixty years old, was doing some kind of yoga.

'Yes?' he questioned, not stopping his exercises. Giorgio explained about the herd, and still raising his legs from the floor and drawing his knees in, the man lifted the phone next to him and informed the farmer who owned them.

'Thanks.' He dismissed them with a wave.

Happy the cows would be alright now, Daisy and Giorgio made their way back to the cabin.

A delicious aroma wafted through the door as they stomped their snow-clagged boots on the mat.

'Hey, that smells great!' Giorgio called from the door.

'Sorry we're later than expected,' Daisy said. 'These white cows had escaped and we wanted to let the farmer know, but all we could find was this weird guy doing yoga in a rickety house.' Daisy laughed. 'Anyway, he phoned the farmer so... well, we're back now.' Daisy had stopped as Grace, who was building the fire up, had her face to the grate and hadn't responded. 'Are you okay?'

'What? Oh, yeah.' Grace rubbed her face. When she turned, it was covered in soot, but it looked very much to Daisy like Grace had been crying.

'Your face is covered in ash,' Giorgio teased. Grace looked at her hands then marched off to wash.

After the meal she'd made, Daisy noticed Grace had barely eaten anything and had gone off to bed early.

'I hope she is okay. She's been rather quiet today,' Daisy observed. 'Do you think she's mad at us for spending so long out?'

Giorgio shrugged then moved closer onto the sofa, watching the flames dance in the hearth. Then he leaned close to Daisy, his lips brushing her cheek. Daisy felt herself melt into his arms and he held her as if he never wanted to let go. She yearned for him to kiss her and moments later felt his warm mouth press firmly against hers, but almost immediately he pulled away. Daisy was confused. Surely she hadn't put him off already? Had she done something wrong? Reading her thoughts, he lifted her chin gently.

'Daisy,' he spoke tenderly, 'I'm worried I'll lose control! You seem to have that effect on me!' Daisy felt herself blush. Would that be so bad? Was he just saying that? Or was it some kind of an excuse?

'I'd better let you go then, for now,' she tried to sound lighthearted but it wasn't how she felt.

Why did he always pull away? It really annoyed her. She thought it was girls who were meant to back off, not boys. Was there something wrong with her that she wanted it to continue? Did she want it to continue? She got up from the sofa. Her body was longing to let things go further but a tiny voice in her mind was questioning this. She felt really frustrated in her body and with her thoughts. How did she really feel about him? Did she want more, really? Or was she just being swept up and about to lose control?

'May as well turn in then,' she said, irritated at her confusion. She hesitated. He could at least come after her. Maybe he really wasn't bothered. She swept through the door, exasperated at his inertia.

That night, Daisy tossed and turned for hours. She'd wanted to talk to Grace but she appeared to be fast asleep, and as she'd seemed a bit quiet earlier Daisy didn't want to disturb her, just in case she wasn't feeling too good. Argh! She wished she could just switch off. She was sick of trying to work out if Giorgio really liked her or not. She wished she could talk to Jonno about this and wondered what he might be doing right now. It must be weird being somewhere different when you woke up every morning. Eventually sleep claimed her, but only for bizarre pictures of harps floating out of her reach to plague her dreams.

Chapter 22 – Disparate Days

Next morning, Daisy woke very early and wrecked with tiredness; she'd had so little sleep. The feelings of frustration flooded back as she woke properly. She looked over at the still sleeping Grace. Daisy couldn't just lie there but it was too dark still to go for a walk. Maybe she'd just get a coffee. She went downstairs and headed for the kettle.

'Hey Daisy.'

'Hi.' Daisy didn't turn. She couldn't look at him. She was still annoyed about last night. She heard him go into the sitting room and made her drink. She should offer him coffee, she thought.

'Do you want a drink?' she called, still not turning.

'Yes, thanks, coffee.'

Daisy took him the cup, thrusting it at him. The hot liquid spilled down the side onto her hand.

'Hey, are you ok?'

She nodded and stalked off to fetch her coffee, closing the kitchen door behind her. Moments later, he came in.

'Daisy?'

'What?'

'Why are you being grumpy? Have I done something to upset you?'

'Not exactly.' She got up to leave.

'Daisy, what's wrong?'

'It's just well, like, last night, you always seem to back

off. I mean, how do you think I feel when that happens?'

'How do you feel?'

'Like there's something wrong with me.'

'I told you, it's not you, it's me. I... I don't want to lose control.'

'Ha! Am I really that tempting? It's like you hardly dare come near me most of the time.'

'Yes. You are.' Giorgio put his head in his hands.

'It's difficult.'

'Huh, there's always some problem. I can't be responsible for how your last girlfriend treated you.' Daisy swept out of the room and back to the bedroom. It was light now; she'd go for a walk. She quietly and quickly threw on her jeans and jumper then grabbed her coat.

'Daisy,' Giorgio called as she went past. She ignored him and left, just remembering not to slam the door as Grace was still asleep.

Daisy took the path towards the farm, stomping along crossly. Minutes later, Giorgio caught her up.

'Hey, hold on please, I want to talk to you. I'll try and explain.' Daisy slowed. 'It's not just that last girl, although she was pretty mean to me after I'd let her know what I thought of her, but I know that you wouldn't be like that.' Daisy stopped and turned to look at him.

'I'm trying to be more open with you but that's not the issue here. I have this cousin...' What was it with him and all these relatives?

'My cousin, Phillipo. He, well, he and this girl,

Christina... she was expecting his child. They were so young, he had a career all lined up for him in his father's business and she had a place at ballet school. He tried to do the right thing, her place was postponed, and he moved away to be with her family so he could help when the baby was born and she could take her ballet place. He couldn't handle it though. He tried to...' Giorgio faltered. Daisy saw tears in his eyes. 'He tried to take his life. She found him. It was terrible. My nonna, gran, took them in as her parents didn't want him there after that, but Phillipo and Christina still wanted to try and raise their little girl. They are doing okay now but it's been very difficult, and I don't want to do that to you or me.'

Daisy nodded. She was probably losing control a bit too. Hard to believe she wanted to push things on when Lucy had all those problems. What was she thinking? It had seemed such a good idea earlier. She just wanted to be closer to him. She wasn't really thinking ahead. She could kind of understand Lucy a bit better now.

'Okay,' she said. He put his arms around her.

'I think you're worth waiting for. I hope you think that about me.'

Daisy blushed. 'I guess. It's just, well, we don't know how long or even if that will be. I don't want this to turn into a "where are we going" convo, but this waiting business... it's not going to be easy.'

He nodded. She sighed.

'Okay, one day at a time. Let's see how Grace is and, well, thank you for explaining all that. I appreciate it.'

They turned back.

Grace was sitting on the steps. Giorgio gestured to Daisy while he went into the cabin.

'Are you okay?' Daisy asked, moving closer.

A robin had come to drink from a little pool of water melting under the porch. Daisy watched as he stuck his head down and tipped it back, letting the water trickle down his back over his brown-grey feathers. He fluttered and shook himself vigorously before settling down to groom his feathery jacket.

'Isn't God's creation awesome?' Grace said,

'I was looking at this little guy and it reminded me of the verse that says God is even concerned about the tiny sparrow. Even if I sometimes forget, I know He cares how I feel and He does have good plans for me.' She shut her eyes. 'It's just, seeing you and Giorgio together, I keep thinking about Oliver. To be honest, I felt really down last night, I couldn't even eat my meal. That happens to me. In fact, I have to watch it a bit. I had a few problems when I was younger. My dad went missing once and, well, that's another story.'

Poor Grace. It was so easy to think other people had it all together, Daisy thought, when really we all have struggles of some sort.

'Oh Grace,' Daisy put her arm around her friend. 'You're amazing. I'm sure Oliver will see that soon. I really am. Giorgio and I, you know, it's just close friends really, there's no way I'd want to make you feel bad. I'm sorry if it's all been a bit in your face. Just throw a cushion at us or something next time.'

Grace laughed.

'You're the best, Daisy! Come on, I'm starving now, let's dig out some cake.'

Chapter 23 – Disarming Days

The next few days at the hut passed quickly. They gathered wood to stack up for Grace's aunt's return and cleaned up. On the last day, Daisy didn't want to leave but she knew it would soon be Christmas, with perhaps a party and then the exchange results. Her heart skipped a beat. She hoped they'd all get a place. There was still today though. She lay dozing until dawn began to break then peeped out of the window. The sunlight glittered through the trees, melting the icicles that dripped outside the window. It looked like it would be a clear day.

A noise beside her caused Daisy to lazily open one eye. She saw Grace slip out of bed, splash water on her face and begin to dress before tiptoeing out of the room. There was packing to do but the three decided to end the day by cooking sausages on a little barbecue.

'I used to do this with my aunt when I was younger, it was fun.' Grace dug out a bag from her coat pocket. 'Marshmallows to melt on sticks for pudding.'

'Hey, go Grace!' Giorgio smacked her on the back.

The bangers and mallows went down a treat and after ensuring the embers in the barbecue were properly out, they called it a night. It would be an early start in the morning.

They were glad to have arrived back at Waterside station after the long journey the following day and joined the throng of people exiting the train. As she stepped down from the carriage, Grace's rucksack strap snapped and her bag began to roll along the platform. Daisy ran to try and catch it.

'I'll get it.' A russet-haired young man stopped to pick it up.

'Thanks,' began Grace catching up, then she stopped. 'Oliver?'

'Grace?' She blushed as he handed her the bag. Daisy thought his sea-green eyes seemed to see her with a new vision. He grinned lopsidedly and said, 'Hi!'

'Hi!' Grace smiled. Daisy hoped the definite interest that registered in his look and his 'hi' meant he finally knew Grace existed as more than a kid. She noticed his hand brushed against Grace's as he passed her the bag.

'Are you walking home?' Oliver asked.

'Yes, these are my friends, Daisy and Giorgio.' Grace introduced them.

'We're just back from the cabin, have you come from uni?'

'Yes, glad to be home.'

As the four of them began the walk back to the village, Oliver grinned at Grace. She looked shyly back then turned but as she did, her bag began to slip again. She reached out to stop it but tripped and fell, landing heavily and yelping in pain as her ankle twisted awkwardly. Daisy went to her, Giorgio ran to get an ice pack from the café, and Oliver lifted her bag carefully away so he could look at her ankle. With the help of her friends, Grace managed to hobble to a taxi that took them to her home, where her paramedic brother diagnosed wrenched ligaments and ordered rest with some light exercise for the next few days.

Daisy sat by her friend.

'I'd been so looking forward to the Christmas party preparations,' Grace began. The party had been okayed earlier.

'I'd mentioned it to Oliver and had hoped he might appear. I won't be up to much dancing now though and this might be the last time I see him for ages if I get a place on the exchange.'

Daisy looked at her friend's gloomy expression, wishing she knew what to say. Grace was so much better at consoling people that she was. Please help, God, she thought.

'Nan's here,' Mrs Bloom called through.

'Hi, Nan. This is Daisy.'

'Nice to meet you.' Grace's nan waved as she walked towards them then bent to hug Grace.

'Now then, what are you like? How's that ankle?'

'It's okay but I'm not. I had all these plans and now I feel as if I'm at a crossroads. I can't even seem to read the signs let alone know which way to go.'

Daisy was intrigued to hear Grace talk to her nan like this. She wondered whether she'd placate her and disappear, like her mum would, or not.

'Sometimes, Grace,' Nan began, 'when you can't see your way forward, look back! You will see the trace of God's hand through your life and He'll always be there even when you can't see Him. He knows your future. I find it's usually the case that if you don't know which way to go, you're in the right place just where you are.'

Grace sighed. 'S'pose.' She gazed out the window. 'Look!' Daisy and Nan turned.

'By the ash trees edging the field near the gnarled trunks and twisted roots, a dog fox!' They saw it come into sight, skulking along the hedge bottom, disturbing the calm and sending birds flying from the hedge in all directions.

'There you are,' said Nan, 'you remember that scripture about little foxes? "Don't get bogged down with things which you really have little control over. Trust in the Lord with all your heart and lean not on your own understanding; in all your ways, submit to Him, and He will make your paths straight."'

Grace nodded.

'I guess I have been thinking God's not moving fast enough for me, but maybe he knows better,' she said reluctantly.

'Is that a bonfire?' Daisy sniffed.

'Yes,' Grace's nan confirmed. 'Your brothers are clearing the field for the party. Why don't you hobble out and look with Daisy?'

'I'll come and look,' said Daisy, 'then I need to head back. I said I'd help Mum a bit tonight as she's having a few friends in for Christmas drinks. I'll be over tomorrow though to help with the preparations.'

Chapter 24 – Day of Dilemma

Daisy lay on her bed later scrolling through Facebook when a message popped up. It was Jonno. "Hi," she messaged back. "Time to chat?" he replied. "Defo." It was ages since she'd spoken to him. She knew he'd been on a long cruise so it would be great to catch up. They messaged back and forth. Jonno told her he was really excited because he and Carlos were both going on a trip to Antarctica with the company. Daisy was really pleased for him. She didn't want to say much about Giorgio and the "waiting conversation", but she told him about the cabin and they talked about the possibility of the exchange. "Maybe we can meet up in NZ if the ship is docking there?" He said he'd look at the schedule and let her know. "I'm back on shift soon. I need to go," he'd finally messaged. "No worries – send me a penguin card!" Daisy sent a penguin icon and signed off. Time for sleep.

She was about to put her phone down when it buzzed again. It was a message on the college Facebook site. The exchange list would be out tomorrow at nine. There was a footnote but Daisy's phone died before she could read it. She stuck it on charge and put her light out.

Next morning, Daisy checked her phone before she even got out of bed. Nothing! It was only seven. She knew she'd have to wait until nine but she kept checking for notifications. Finally, at nine exactly, a notification popped onto her screen. She scanned the list. Grace

Bloom – yes. Giorgio Chrisodoulous – yes. She scanned the Ds for Davidson. She scanned again and again, up and down the list, in case it had somehow been placed out of alphabetical order. No. It wasn't there.

She threw the phone across the bed. Waves of self pity welled up, resentment foaming as they crashed angrily through her mind. Typical, just typical. Why was she always the one not chosen? Grace and Giorgio would be so pleased. She reached down the bed and picked up the phone. "Congratulations," she texted. "My phone is about to die," she lied, "catch you later." She turned her phone off and flopped back on the bed, burying her head in the pillow.

She felt so isolated. She didn't want to go to the party now or help with the preps. They'd all be celebrating Giorgio and Grace getting a place. Why did these things happen to her? Why for once, just once, couldn't she be chosen too? It was mean. That would mean someone else missing out. She was pleased for Giorgio and Grace, but so disappointed for herself. She wouldn't be able to face them. She didn't want to let Grace down over the party but definitely couldn't bear to go. What could she do? She banged her head on her pillow, tears stinging in her eyes. Giorgio would probably meet some gorgeous girl out there now and forget about her.

She reached up to her bedside table for Ted. Mum was always moving him off her bed, which really annoyed her. Her hand grazed the little Bible but she didn't pick it up. She felt really jealous of her friends and hated this feeling. She was pleased for them, of course, but why couldn't it be her too? She felt cross with God as well. How could he let them go and not her? The tears fell. Daisy put her head under the covers and sobbed until she fell asleep again.

Muddle woke her a while later. He wanted a walk and she was the only one in as the rest of the family had gone Christmas shopping. Good job she'd done hers online. She was in no mood for Christmas now. The day seemed even greyer as she sat up to draw the curtains. She dragged herself out of bed, dressed and picked up her phone. She couldn't bear to turn it on though. She didn't want to see any pity texts. She wouldn't be able to give Giorgio his gift if she didn't go to help prepare the party. Tears threatened again but determinedly she clipped on Muddle's lead and went out and towards the lane.

The last of the leaves fluttered onto her as she brushed past the trees by the gate. Moments later, Muddle pulled on the lead and looking up she saw he'd spotted Grace's dogs. Hastily she turned into a small hedged paddock. Muddle slid under the line of barbed wire. She hurriedly tried to climb over it but caught her leg. Dragging it away, she crouched out of sight, feeling warm blood seeping through her now ripped jeans. Good job they weren't her best ones. Muddle was occupying himself with digging a mole hill and thankfully he didn't appear to notice when they approached. She heard Grace and Oliver talking excitedly about New Zealand. Bile rose in her throat.

Suddenly, Muddle realised his pals were there and

shot out, his lead slipping Daisy's grasp. She wanted to avoid them but knew there was no way she could do that now, not if she still valued her friendship with Grace. She emerged, struggling to control her urge to turn back as they saw her and waved. Grace was still hobbling.

'How's the foot?' Daisy asked as they joined her. She could at least ask about that, she decided.

'Mending, thanks. I'm supposed to exercise it a bit. Oliver's helping,' Grace said, grinning. 'Great news about the trip, isn't it?'

'Yes, er, amazing for you and Giorgio.' Daisy forced the words out.

'For you too,' said Oliver.

Daisy stared at him. What was he on about? In what world did he think it was good news for her? How could not going possibly be good news for her? What did it have to do with him anyway? Daisy bit her lip and looked at the ground. She wanted to scream at him but she didn't want to upset Grace.

'Daisy?' Grace questioned.

'Sorry, bit of a rush, need to get Muddle back,' Daisy muttered and sped off.

'Er, see you later to prep for the party,' Grace called after her. Daisy couldn't answer. She gave a wave and hurried on.

What should she do now? She would have to go. How would she control her feelings though? She didn't want to get mad or cry or behave like a jerk in some way. Daisy began to run as she battled with her feelings. She really wanted to help with the party preparation. Why did she worry so much about betraying her feelings? Why couldn't she just get over herself?

Arriving home, she unclipped Muddle and flung his lead into the porch. She dragged off her wellies and headed upstairs to her room. Daisy looked at herself in her mirror. Okay, so she would go. She was fed up with allowing her emotions to dictate her social life, she informed her reflection most sternly, but her eyes gave away the internal terror.

'Okay,' she continued, whispering now as she didn't want anyone to hear her talking to her reflection, 'I know you're scared, but come on – these are your friends. Surely you can find some way of being among them without some emo crisis, even if you are feeling gutted at the NZ list not including you.' Her eyes told her she seemed less terrified now.

So what could she do if she began to feel overwhelmed later? Her mind whizzed virtually around the Broom's farmhouse, which she now knew almost as well as her own. The attic room – of course! She was staying over after the party so it would be fine to escape there on the pretence of putting her things up in the room. Okay, so she could probably manage to hold it together then. She nodded at herself, gathered all she would need and set off.

Chapter 25 – Daisy's Determined

Giorgio was already there when Daisy arrived, helping Grace's brother put up some fairylights. He had a roll of Sellotape in his mouth and was on top of a ladder. Seeing Daisy, he took a hand off the ladder to give her a wave. The house looked amazing in festive gold but it was nearly five. Not much time to complete the finishing touches. Grace was having a panic over the entertainment so Daisy went to help the boys. Giorgio hung the last of the lights while she held the ladder, then joined her to rearrange the chairs.

'So, about the NZ trip,' he began. Daisy put her hand to her head.

'Sorry, need to ask Grace something.' She sped upstairs, grabbing her bag on the way. In the attic room, she lay face-down on the bed.

'I can't do this,' she told the pillow, 'I just can't. God, what am supposed to say?' The door opened and she lifted her head. Grace stood in the doorway, looking at her quizzically.

'Giorgio said you had something to ask me?' Daisy groaned.

'What's up?'

She dropped her eyes.

'It's, er, well, it's the NZ trip. I mean, I'm pleased for you guys but...'

'Oh, of course,' Grace said with sudden realisation,

'your phone died. I bet you haven't checked the list recently. Your name was up as a reserve. You know the footnote said, "Confirmation to be sent by return and any named persons who've had a change of mind are to notify the college immediately and there will be a reposting if needed at 12 noon." Anyway, apparently someone had a change of mind once they got a place and you were next on the list.'

Daisy shook her head in disbelief. She'd never read the footnote.

'It's true,' Oliver countered, sticking his head in.

'How do you know?' she questioned.

'I know because I put the names up,' Oliver replied, 'I'm the link with Christchurch School. It's part of my outdoor leadership dissertation.'

'Who knew?' Grace laughed, nodding. She thrust her phone at Daisy.

'Check it out.'

Daisy looked at the screen, back at Grace, and then at the screen again.

'Yaaaaaaay! I can hardly believe it. Oh wow, this is amazing! Does Giorgio know this?' Grace hugged her friend.

'Sure he does. He was just saying he was about to discuss it with you when you rushed off to ask me something.'

'Wow, this is amazing! I must check I can go so I can confirm. Is it okay if I go home and check?'

'Of course.'

'Great. I'll be back ASAP.'

Once home, Daisy dashed through the back door into the kitchen, nearly colliding with Nan. 'Nan, Nan, I've got a place! On the NZ trip! I'm going, I'm really going. This is amazing!' She hesitated. 'As long as Mum and Dad let me...' She looked up at Nan.

'Come on, let's go and see.'

'Well, we knew you'd applied but we didn't imagine you would get a place. What about the cost?' her parents asked.

'It's an exchange trip.' Daisy tried to keep her voice even. 'All costs are covered by the Exchange Fund except spending money.'

'Where do you stay?'

'In student accommodation near the college. It's catered.'

'How much spending money are you expected to take and where are you going to find that?'

'Er...' Daisy could feel panic rising. Surely her parents wouldn't stop her going? She must keep her temper and show them she was an adult. Her throat felt dry and her heart was thrashing around as if it wanted to jump out and let them see how important this was to her. She took a breath.

'A thousand pounds is recommended, but I'm sure I can ...' She stopped, seeing her parents swap glances, both with the look that said, "This isn't happening then."

Daisy put her hand to her mouth. Sick – she was going

to be sick. She mustn't leave the room though. They'd think she was storming off. Inhale, exhale, inhale, exhale, she told herself. She'd never believed those breathing exercises in the Wellbeing Class would pay off but incredibly the nausea dissipated. She decided to sit down and as she did, Nan piped up.

'Oh, that's sorted. I have been putting a little aside into a savings account for the girls from their birth and this is just the kind of adventure it was meant for. There will still be plenty left for university or a house deposit as well.'

'Really?' Her parents said in unison.

'Thank you, Nan.' Daisy hugged her fiercely.

After that, it was just details. Daisy could barely take them in. She felt hot then cold as adrenalin coursed through her. It was so totally amazing! Finally, it was agreed. She could confirm. She sent up a prayer of gratitude.

'Oh,' she added, 'I was so angry with you earlier, sorry about that. You had it all worked out. I guess I still need to work on trusting you even when things don't look great. I can't believe I'm going... This is brilliant! I'm so looking forward to the party now.'

Daisy looked at herself in the mirror. She had on her new black jeans and a white top with stars glittering along the neckline. Not bad. She grinned at herself. She picked up her overnight bag to go but her phone buzzed twice. There was a message from the jazz group: "There's a surprise gig – will fill you in shortly." Hope it's after Christmas, she thought. The other message was from

Jonno. She messaged back. "How are you doing? Just off to a party, will text later. Love Daze xx"

Chapter 26 – Dynamic Days

Daisy raced back to the Bloom's but stopped to take a moment to compose herself, brushing back stray strands of hair that had escaped from her hairclip as she'd run. Giorgio was in the kitchen when she arrived.

'Hey, congratulations on your exchange place, so cool that we all get to go,' he said, hugging her.

'Waiter time!' He grinned, picking up a tray of mugs steaming with fragrant mulled wine and headed off.

When Daisy went into the sitting room, she was surprised to see Mrs Stringer and Grace's brother, Zach.

'Hi. Great to see you, didn't know you'd be here!'

'We've just been invited – to play. This is the surprise gig.'

Mrs Stringer gestured to the corner and Daisy went hot and cold as she saw the harp she usually played.

'The original group backed out at the last minute – sick bug or something – so Grace called us!' Mrs Stringer headed off to check the mics.

Daisy's mouth went dry and she felt sick again.

You can't play! a voice screamed in her head. Not this – you're too new to it. Not in front of Giorgio, the whole Bloom family and your friends. They'll think you are actually ridiculous.

What if you don't play? What then? another small voice questioned. No music for the party – your friends will be let down and it will be embarrassing for the jazz trio. What's more important to you; helping out or your pride? Daisy gulped. She knew the answer but her courage had taken a hike.

'Are you okay?' Phil asked. Daisy began to nod and then shook her head.

'Nervous,' she muttered.

'First time you've played in front of friends?' She nodded.

'I know the feeling,' Phil continued, 'happened to me last Christmas, but it'll be fine once you begin, trust me. We'll only be playing the Christmas songs we've been practising and only two sets of twenty minutes.'

Daisy sighed. No-one except Jonno knew she'd been practising the jazz harp. She hadn't wanted to tell even Giorgio and Grace until she felt competent, as she knew they'd want to hear her play and she just hadn't felt ready. For her, playing in front of people was like opening her heart, and it filled her with dread.

You managed to hold it together when you discussed the NZ trip with your parents, a quiet voice in her head reminded her.

Grace came into the room. 'Guess what? Dad has been given leave for New Year! He'll be home on the 30th for a week!' Grace tore across to her brothers to tell them the good family news.

Celebrations were definitely called for and Daisy didn't want to be the one to halt them. She wasn't sure where Giorgio was but decided if she was going to do this thing and play, she'd better get organised with the harp while her friends were both distracted elsewhere. Her hands shook as she positioned her instrument. Hopefully Phil was right and once she began... Her heart raced as if it was full of huge dragonflies about to leap out of her, then the trio began playing. Daisy, who knew the songs by heart, shut her eyes to begin with so she wouldn't have to look at everyone.

After the first medley, there was a round of applause and she opened her eyes to see Giorgio and Grace looking at her with surprised admiration, clapping wildly. Daisy swallowed hard. A bubble of pride welled up. No-one was laughing at her. Perhaps she could do this performing thing after all? In fact, she was almost looking forward to the next medley already.

Between sets, Daisy had a bit of explaining to do. Giorgio had thought she'd dipped out of time with him to catch up on work, but it had definitely been worth it. She felt like a tree whose branches had begun to stretch out in the spring sunshine.

Later, much later, she and Grace headed up to bed. She felt elated and exhausted, but before she let her head touch the pillow, Daisy grabbed her phone and remembered to text Jonno. "Hi, sorry it took a while to message back. Hope you're okay. Today has been amazing for me. It started like crap but now it's brilliant. Can you believe I have a place on the exchange! I didn't at first but then someone dropped out and I was next on the list. So let me know if you're going to be in NZ at all between January and April because I will be!!! I hope we can meet up.

I'm so excited. Also, that party I mentioned, a party with friends I didn't even know I'd have when we first arrived here, it turned out the jazz trio I play with were dragged in last minute when the original band let them down and I PLAYED THE JAZZ HARP – in front of them all! ME – can you believe that? See, I am following my dreams – I haven't let them go. I can't believe I didn't want to be here and now I don't want to leave. Well, only to go to NZ! It's like I'm looking at a different world, or maybe it's me that's different? Love Daze xx"

www.ingramcontent.com/pod-product-compliance
Lightning Source LLC
Chambersburg PA
CBHW011442170626
46807CB00009B/3275